THE
THE GO

THE TEMPLE OF THE GOLDEN HORDE

MICHAEL COLLINS

(writing as Robert Hart Davis)

WILDSIDE PRESS

THE TEMPLE OF THE GOLDEN HORDE
A Charlie Chan Mystery

Originally published in *Charlie Chan Mystery Magazine*, May 1974. Copyright © 1974 by Renown Publishing Company. This version copyright © 2002 by David Linds. All rights reserved.

Published by:
Wildside Press
P.O. Box 301
Holicong, PA 18928-0301
www.wildsidepress.com

I

A THIN FOG hung over the high iron gates of the isolated estate on Half Moon Bay south of San Francisco. The night was chill and silent, and for a long time nothing moved among the trees and the dark, distant buildings behind the high fence. The only sound was the muffled churning of surf on rocks far off in the fog.

Somewhere the faint chimes of a clock struck ten times through the mist, when a pickup truck came out of the fog along the narrow dirt road and screeched to a halt outside the high iron gates. A small Chinese man jumped out. For a moment he stood there between the pickup and the high gates as if not sure what to do next.

He wore baggy old corduroy pants, a denim shirt, a dark blue windbreaker, and worn, dirty sneakers. There was something vacant about his smooth Oriental face, which had the almost puzzled expression of a child, but on the thin body of a man in his early thirties. He carried a brass-bound chest of dark wood, about the size of a bowling-ball bag, and he looked around apprehensively.

Suddenly his head cocked like a nervous bird ready to fly. He seemed to hear something in the night; blinking down at the small chest in his hands, he ran to a small side gate beside the high iron gates, unlocked it with a key, went through, and slammed it shut behind him.

Once more he stood and listened, smiling broadly as if all at once feeling happy, and he began to walk up a curving gravel drive toward a large fog-shrouded building some half a mile ahead. He walked in quick, short steps, half-running with one leg almost dragging in a sideways movement like a hurrying crab.

The building loomed before him. One of three structures scattered some distance apart on the wooded grounds, it was nothing at all like the other two. Where they were ordinary two-story yellow stucco buildings in a Spanish style, this one was all dark wood and tile with an open porch that ran around all four sides. Wooden pillars held up a high red-lacquered roof like a curved pyramid whose the corners had been turned up—a Chinese pagoda in the mist of the California shore.

Eagerly, the small Chinese man hurried toward the tall pagoda with his crab-like steps. Then he stopped.

His child-like face became a mask of sheer terror. He stumbled backwards in the gravel drive, still clutching the brass-bound wooden chest.

They seemed to rise up out of the ground, out of the fog itself, between the small Chinese man and the dark, eerie pagoda. Six shapes like wraiths in the mist, blending gray into the swirling night, faceless and silent, gliding soundlessly as if their feet did not touch the earth.

With a low, moaning cry, the small Chinese man turned and ran toward where the trees thinned. He fled wildly, in panic, not looking back. As he reached the last trees, the fog thickened, and he began to stumble over hummocks of grass. Twice he fell, but he got up and ran on, still clinging to the brass-bound box.

A new sound filled the night.

The sound of the ocean on rocks.

A close sound growing louder.

The fleeing man stopped.

He looked behind him in fear—and ahead of him in terror.

The hooded figures drifted around him, closing in on all sides. Ahead of where the small Chinese man stood shaking, the dark, surging ocean broke on a rocky beach.

The small Chinese man's childlike face collapsed into something not quite human. The brass-bound chest slipped from his fingers to the rocks and sand. The inrushing tide lapped closer.

Whimpering like some small, hopeless animal, he began to back away from the water. Then he turned and saw the six demonic shapes encircling him.

He stood as if paralyzed, only his mouth moving, making low, animal moans of fear.

The six hooded figures closed around him, and he screamed.

II

THE WINTER SUN broke through the morning fog of San Francisco just before noon and streamed into a luxurious suite at The Mark Hopkins. A pair of Peking nightingales hopping happily in a cylindrical cage hanging near the windows greeted the sudden brightness with song.

"Ah," a portly Chinese gentleman said as he approached the stand from which the cage of singing birds hung, "lucky is the man whose day begins with the song of small birds."

Dressed in an impeccable dark suit under a silk Chinese robe, Charlie Chan crooned to the two birds, then fed them some choice seeds. His pale ivory face smiled under his thin mustache, and his ample body had the fluid motion of a man without fat despite his portliness.

The ringing of the suite's telephone interrupted

his pleasant moment with his birds. Sighing, the famous detective answered the insistent instrument.

"Yes," he said, "this is Inspector Chan of the Honolulu Police. . . . I am most grateful for your official welcome. . . . I have no need of assistance. I will be at the afternoon meeting as arranged. . . . Thank you."

Chan hung up with a faint smile at the eager public relations man's welcoming call. A smile that turned into a frown as the great detective reflected on the way the whole world was being run by public relations men who greeted a complete stranger like a long lost brother simply because he was an "important person."

The International Penology Symposium he had come to San Francisco to attend was a serious gathering of criminology experts from across the world, but it would accomplish nothing if it was turned into a circus of "celebrities" such as himself. With a resigned sigh, Chan crossed the suite to a desk. He sat down and began to read through a thin manuscript of the speech he was scheduled to give at the first symposium this afternoon. He was to precede Prefect DeBevre of Paris.

Chan was still going over his speech half an hour later when he heard odd footsteps out in the hotel corridor.

With no outward signs, Chan came alert. The reflex awareness of every tiny change around him stemmed from his long years of police work and was automatic by now. Without moving a hair, he listened.

The footsteps outside his suite were quick, yet tentative. They were the light steps of a woman who was unsure of herself, even nervous. Diffident, or else trying to be unheard as she moved closer.

Chan did not hesitate. Soundlessly, he stood and glided to the door. He listened almost without breathing, his dark, hooded eyes half closed. The footsteps came on, soft and light—and stopped at his door.

Chan rested his hand on his pistol under his robe and reached for the doorknob.

There was a hesitant knock, and then a little stronger as if the woman were forcing courage. Chan opened the door.

"Inspector Charlie Chan?"

She was a small, slender Chinese girl in her early twenties. Her face was as pale as new ivory, but there was a spirit to it, her dark eyes sharp and bright. Not an old-fashioned Chinese girl, but one of the modern Chinese-American kind. As if to prove this, she wore a thoroughly American dark green sweater and a short swinging skirt. Chan bowed, smiling.

"Of the Honolulu Police, yes," he said. "Please come in. I am honored by this visit of a distant countrywoman so young and so pretty."

The girl flushed at the compliment, but she

stepped into the suite, looking around curiously as if wondering how a famous detective lived. For a moment, the liveliness of her youth overcame whatever was making her pale and uneasy. Chan waved her to a seat.

"A glass of wine, perhaps?" Chan asked gently.

"What?" She seemed startled for a second, then sat down. She shook her head, refusing the offered wine, and sat with her knees tightly together as if suddenly remembering what trouble had brought her to Chan. "You . . . you're the real Charlie Chan? I mean, you're the famous detective?"

"Oh yes," Chan said with a smile. "I am Charlie Chan, Chief of Honolulu Detectives, and a very ancient policeman. That much is true."

"Mr. Chan, it's my brother! He—"

Chan held up his hand. "All journeys start with the first step. What is your name, young lady?"

The girl took a deep breath, "I'm sorry. My name is Chan, too, Inspector. Betty Chan of San Francisco. I've lived here all my life. That's why, when I read in the paper you were in town, I decided to come to you. My—"

"To meet an unknown member of my family is like discovering a rare new rose in my garden. You are the daughter of what Chan?"

"My father was Chan Wu Han, Inspector. He was no one important, a waiter in Chinatown. He died when I was a child."

"Ah, I do remember your father. He was a waiter in the Kung Shi Restaurant. I was served by him once many years ago. At the time he had only a son."

"You do remember him!" the girl said, amazed and for an instant smiling back. Then her face darkened again. "Yes, he had one son, older than I am. My brother Benny. Now he's dead, Inspector! Benny is dead."

"I'm sorry." Chan said sympathetically.

"Perhaps he's better off dead, Mr. Chan," the girl said bitterly, "but he was all I had."

"His death was recent?"

"He disappeared four days ago, Inspector. Yesterday they found him in Half Moon Bay. He'd drowned." She looked up at Chan. "The police say it was an accident, but I know that Benny was murdered!"

Chan sat down facing the girl. "That is a grave charge, Miss Chan. You have some reason to suggest the police are mistaken?"

"I know Benny didn't drown by accident!" The pretty young girl glared at Chan.

The detective showed no reaction, his dark eyes watched her. "You know of some one who wished your brother dead?"

"No, I don't. Benny wasn't important, just a handyman at the Temple of the Golden Horde. It's a kind of religious cult down on Half Moon Bay south of here. The Khan—he runs the temple—was always very good to Benny. Benny lived down there. He was never in any trouble, but—"

"You know, then, of some motive for murder, Miss Chan?"

She shook her head. "No, Benny never hurt anyone."

"You have, then, some evidence his death was not an accident as the police say?"

"No, I don't!" Betty Chan cried. "All I know is that Benny couldn't have drowned unless someone drowned him!"

Chan sat back thoughtfully, frowning. "The police are most skilled in matters of murder, Miss Chan. They make few mistakes, and without a shred of proof to the contrary, a wise man must agree with them. I suggest—"

"They may know murder, Mr. Chan," Betty Chan said hotly, "but they didn't know Benny the way I did!" And then her eyes began to fill with tears where she sat with her knees pressed so tightly together. "He . . . he wasn't very bright, Inspector Chan. Before he went to work for the Temple, I took care of him. He wasn't crazy or anything, but . . ."

"Go on," Chan said.

She looked up. "The truth is that Benny was retarded, Mr. Chan. Not very badly, but enough to have the mind of maybe a twelve-year-old boy. He could take care of himself day to day, but he couldn't plan things or think of the future, and the best job he ever had before the Temple was as a messenger."

She was crying harder now, but without a sound, the tears flowing down her pretty young face. Chan watched her, but said nothing. She was talking out her pain, he knew, and it was best to let her release it all her own way.

"I loved Benny, he was so gentle," she said through her tears, "but it was hard to take care of him, so when the Temple offered him the handyman's job, it was a godsend. Benny loved the Temple. He was very religious-minded, and he loved the Khan and his work down there. He felt actually needed, responsible, and that was important to Benny. He knew he wasn't like other men, so to have real importance gave him great pride and a great sense of duty. Do you understand, Mr. Chan?"

Chan nodded. "You are saying that Benny would never commit suicide. From your description, I must agree such men do not kill themselves. But such men do have many accidents, Miss Chan."

"No, Inspector, they don't. They're super careful, always afraid, and they never take any chances."

"Still, this Temple of the Golden Horde, is it on a bay? Perhaps very close to the water?" Chan asked. "A dark night, a man walks unknowingly too close to the edge? Could your brother swim, Miss Chan? Such men usually—"

"No, Benny couldn't swim, not a stroke," Betty Chan said.

"Then it is possible—"

"It is impossible that Benny drowned by accident," the girl said, interrupted. "Benny saw a friend drown when he was in his teens, and he never got over it. He never went near water again. He couldn't swim, wouldn't even go on a beach or in a boat, hated even to come near a bridge. You see, Mr. Chan, Benny had a pathological fear of water!"

Chan scrutinized her young face. She had all but stopped crying now, her eyes set in a firm certainty that her brother's death had not been an accident.

"Of this you are certain?" Chan said at last.

"Yes," Betty Chan said. "Benny could never have gone near the ocean. He couldn't have ever been close enough to fall in by accident. Will you . . . investigate, Mr. Chan?"

Chan thought for a time. Then he nodded. "There would appear to be enough doubt to raise questions. You have said you know of no enemies, no reason for murder. But did your brother do any unusual act recently? Did he speak to you of any fears or dangers?"

"No, nothing. On the night he vanished, he'd just come back from Honolulu on an errand for the Khan at the Temple. He never made it back to the Temple."

"Can you name the nature of the errand?"

"Just to pick up some kind of scroll and bring it to the Khan at the Temple."

"This scroll, did it vanish, too?"

"No, I don't think so."

Chan nodded. "I'll need the location of the Temple."

Betty Chan told him how to reach the temple on Half Moon Bay and gave him the name of Lieutenant Forbes of the Highway Patrol barrack at Half Moon Bay as the man in charge of the case.

"You'll go now, Inspector?"

"No, but soon. First I have a speech to give early this afternoon, and then I must consider the best course of action," Chan said. He smiled and stood up to go, touching Betty on her thin shoulder. "An answer will be found. It is best now that you rest. Remember, the life of a young woman must come before the sorrow of what is passed."

Betty Chan nodded, stood up. "I'll try, Mr. Chan, and thank you. I . . . I only want to know how Benny really died, and why."

III

BETTY CHAN went out of the suite slowly, her head down as if the weight of her brother rested on her. Chan watched the door close thoughtfully. She seemed a steady young woman, and yet the police were rarely wrong in such matters. With another sigh, and a glance at the manuscript of his speech, he crossed the sunny room to the windows above the steep San Francisco street.

His nostrils flared slightly, and he smiled at himself—the scent of a chase interested the great detective far more than a dull speech to yawning colleagues. He thought about a retarded man afraid of water who 'accidentally' drowned, and . . .

Chan stared down at the San Francisco street. The slim figure of Betty Chan came out of the hotel and crossed the street. She walked quickly downhill toward the center of the city.

She didn't walk alone.

Two men walked after her. They were casual, seeming to pay no attention to the girl, but Chan had been a policeman too long not to know better. They had appeared as if by magic from a doorway across the steep street, followed too casually, seemed too unconcerned, and when Betty Chan turned at the end of the block, both of them walked faster, almost running, and followed her around the corner.

It was too far for Chan to see their faces—just two men in neutral gray suits and hats, carrying folded newspapers, trying to look like everyone else in the city. But he was sure they were following Betty Chan.

The detective turned from the window, removed his robe, put on his suit coat and light topcoat, picked up his speech, and left the suite. He went down to the hotel dining room for some lunch, ordering the abalone sauteed with slivered almonds, a California delicacy. At precisely one P.M. he finished his second cup of special Chinese tea, and walked from the hotel into an afternoon beginning to cloud over and with a sharp wind rising up from the great bay.

Something moved in the same doorway. where the two men had come from to follow Betty Chan. A faint movement, but clear to Chan's practiced eye. Someone had shifted, come alert, as if seeing what he had been waiting for.

Without the slightest hesitation or breaking of his stride, Chan turned left down the street, giving no indication that he had seen anything at all. He walked briskly in the rising wind, but did not hurry, pausing twice to look at especially striking examples of the bay window construction of so many San Francisco town houses. Each time he was careful not to look behind him.

He turned the same corner Betty Chan had earlier, quickened his pace, and this time he did look behind as he stopped to glance at a shop window.

A tall, lean man in a brown suit came hurrying around the corner, saw Charlie Chan, and with the slightest of hesitations, crossed the street at an angle and went on past Chan. Just a hint of surprise and hesitation, a trained follower, but Chan had not missed the brief instant.

The man was following him!

He waited until the tall man turned the far corner, then he retraced his steps to the street of the hotel, and turned downhill toward the heart of the city. At the first hidden doorway, Chan slipped inside and waited. If his shadower was as good as he seemed, he shouldn't have lost Chan yet. Chan waited for the tall man to come along in pursuit.

After ten minutes the tall man did not appear. No one appeared following him.

The tall man was, perhaps, even better than

Chan had expected; too trained to fall into the trap of being caught by a man he was tailing.

Chan stepped out of his doorway, hailed a taxi, and sat back to ride the few blocks to the hotel where his International Symposium was taking place. But he was thinking about the men who seemed so interested in Betty Chan and now in him.

*   *   *

It was growing dark as Charlie Chan drove south in the rented dark-blue Toyota. He was a careful driver and never really felt at home behind the wheel of any car except the immaculate 1949 Cadillac sedan now waiting sedately back in his driveway on Punchbowl Hill in Honolulu.

His speech had gone well, there had been a long discussion session that promised productive work for the rest of the week, and Chan was feeling satisfied—except for the small voice at the back of his mind still wondering about the death of Benny Chan, and about the men tailing Betty Chan and himself. But those were questions that would, perhaps, soon be answered.

He drove with the sound of the ocean to his right, and entered Half Moon Bay just after six o'clock. The Highway Patrol barrack stood off the roadway of Route One, a pleasant building designed to blend into the wooded countryside. Chan parked and went in to ask for Lieutenant Forbes. The desk sergeant yawned.

"Lieutenant's pretty busy," he said. "You better tell me your business. First, what's your name, and what's the trouble?"

"Inspector Chan, Honolulu Police Department," Chan said quietly. "My business is with Lieutenant—"

"Chan?" the desk sergeant gaped, stood up. "Charlie Chan? The real Charlie Chan? I mean— Hey, I've read all about you! Wow. I mean . . . I'll get the lieutenant."

The sergeant spoke into his desk telephone, and moments later a short, heavy man in civilian clothes came hurrying along a corridor. He held his hand out to Chan.

"Inspector Chan!" the heavy man exclaimed. "I'm Harry Forbes. The captain was just talking about you. He was up at the symposium and heard your speech. You've got him all excited."

"I'm glad he was interested," Chan said sincerely.

"Well," Lt. Forbes said, "excited is probably an understatement. You wanted to talk to me?"

"A few moments of your time would be welcome," Chan said politely.

"Sure, sure! Come on in."

The short man led Chan back along the corridor to a cluttered private office. He closed the door, waved Chan to a chair, and sat back, beaming at the famous detective.

"What can I do for you, Inspector Chan?"

"I have come concerning the death of Benny Chan."

"Benny Chan?" Forbes frowned. "Oh, yeah, the handyman over at the Temple of the Golden Horde. Drowned, a lousy accident. Chan, yeah? Was he a relative of yours?" Forbes asked.

"Perhaps distant, but unknown to me. Yet all Chans are of the same family, and Benny Chan's sister has requested my assistance. Purely unofficial, of course, but I would appreciate—"

Forbes shook his head. "She was here, too. The sister says Benny was murdered, but we've got absolutely no evidence of murder. Who would want to kill Benny?"

"You knew him well?"

"Everyone around Half Moon Bay knew Benny. He was always in town on errands for the Temple people. About the only one from the Temple we saw much of. The rest of them out there keep pretty much to themselves. Some of the local parents didn't like Benny around, but he was harmless. We checked him out years ago. He was never in any trouble, shy and always helpful."

"What can you tell me of the Temple and its people?"

"Not much. Some sort of Oriental cult, and a kind of rest home and training center. Like I said, they keep to themselves, the place is fenced, no one gets in without an invitation. It's run by a Chinese man named Li Po, calls himself the Khan, and his wife. Don't know her real name—calls herself the Snow Princess. A lawyer named Sedgwick runs their business affairs, and they never cause any trouble, either."

"The members of this cult are not local? Do they live there?"

"Some do, sort of like a Catholic 'retreat house' it seems, but they come from all over, mostly San Francisco. On weekends." Forbes lit a battered pipe, blew thick smoke. "Benny Chan's been here maybe five years. That sister was never here before as far as I know, doesn't belong to the cult. I figure we know Benny maybe better than she does, and if he was murdered, I can't see any reason."

"She was close to her retarded brother in spirit if not in locality."

"Well, maybe," Forbes said, "but she couldn't give us any motive—or she wouldn't."

Chan said, "Wouldn't? You think she has hidden knowledge?"

"Could be she's involved in something up in San Francisco she thinks might have gotten Benny killed, but doesn't want us to know about it. How well do you know her, Inspector?"

"I met her the first time today," Chan admitted, and he had to think about the men he'd seen tailing Betty Chan and, later, himself—if they were the same group of men. "The night of Benny Chan's accident, were strangers perhaps seen or reported in the area?"

"None that I heard about," Forbes said. "Of course, a lot of this area is pretty isolated, especially along the coast. I can dig into it deeper if you think it's important."

"It could be," Chan said. "I do not wish to interfere, but I hope to put the mind of his sister to rest. I would also like to view the body, if possible, and examine the effects of Benny Chan."

"Anything you want, Inspector. If we missed something, we sure want to know about it. But, honestly, I don't see much doubt about the accident."

"I am sure you are correct," Chan said quietly. "But his unhappy sister will pace the cage of uncertainty until all avenues of doubt are closed. The shadow of uncertainly must be raised from her young life."

"Come on then," Forbes said. "Benny's down in the Coroner's morgue at the sub-station. I'll drive you."

*   *   *

The Sheriff's Sub-Station was off the main street of Half Moon Bay. The morgue was in the basement. A white-coated attendant pulled out one of the six drawers, and Chan looked down at the bloated body of Benny Chan.

"In the water three days, the Coroner says," Lieutenant Forbes said. "Death was definitely by drowning, alive when he went into the water. From where we found the body, we're pretty sure he entered the ocean somewhere near the Temple. The currents are just right for where we found him. No other marks on the body except the usual battering of the rocks. He was fully dressed, and nothing seemed to be missing from his pockets."

Chan examined the body briefly, stared for a moment at the water swollen face that seemed to have a small smile on it. A boyish face, as if the face belonged to a child and not a full-grown man. The detective turned to the pitiful collection of personal effects. They had been in the water. The wallet had partially disintegrated, but nothing seemed gone. There were even a few dollar bills, Benny Chan's identity card, some keys, loose change, and a moth-eaten rabbit's foot.

Chan's eyes surveyed them.

"Even the sister admits that's about all Benny ever carried," Lieutenant Forbes said, "and the people at the Temple know of nothing valuable Benny could have had."

Chan read the Coroner's report—death by drowning, water in the lungs, abrasions and contusions from contact with rocks and sand after death. He went once more to study the body, bending to examine the cuts and scrapes.

"I see there are bruises on the back of his neck," Chan said slowly. "Also on his arms above the elbows and wrists. Difficult places for rocks to bruise, and not accompanied by cuts or abrasions."

"Floating debris, maybe," Forbes said. "Logs, wood."

"Perhaps, but the bruises on each arm and wrist are in the exact same places, almost exact size, and deep, as if pressure was exerted." Chan continued to stare down at the small bruises on the dead man's arms and wrists. "As if he was held by the arms and neck, by more than one man. Head held under water until he drowned."

"Without any evidence, that's a pretty wild guess, Mr. Chan," Forbes said. "When a man's been in the sea three days, it's a thousand-to-one the bruises come from the bottom. Besides, it isn't easy to drown a man, not when he's conscious. He'd have struggled like all hell, and there'd be more marks."

"Unless he was paralyzed by fear," Chan said softly. "You are sure nothing was stolen from Benny Chan?"

"We're sure," Forbes said. "Seen enough, Inspector?"

"For now," Chan said.

They went up and out to Forbes's car and drove back to the Highway Patrol barrack. As they entered Forbes's private office, an elderly Chinese man jumped up from where he had been sitting.

"My scroll, Lieutenant, where is it?" His voice was soft but agitated. "Where is the Scroll of Batu Khan!"

IV

HE WAS A TALL, bone-thin Chinese man with an aged, dignified face trimmed by a long white mustache that drooped to his chin in ancient Chinese fashion. In his mid-sixties, he wore a spartan black robe of pure silk, simple sandals, and had the erect dignity of a simple Oriental monk.

Before Lieutenant Forbes could answer, Chan stepped forward, spoke quietly and with a small bow:

"Unexpected honor for traveler in distant place to greet scholar and famed benefactor from home," the detective said in Mandarin.

The dignified old man seemed to see Chan for the first time. His thin face broke into a smile. "Why, Inspector Chan! I am the one who is honored. Humble dilettante of ancient culture must bow to greater fame of Charlie Chan." His dark eyes seemed to sparkle. "You have, then, located priceless scroll?"

Forbes said, "You two know each other?"

"Mr. C.V. Soong," Chan introduced the aristocratic old man to Forbes. "Great historian of all things Chinese, a noted scholar, benefactor, and philanthropist."

"Value of wealth only measured by deeds for those in need," C.V. Soong said. "To be buried in riches is a crime. Money taken from world by industrious father must be returned to world."

"Not all men of wealth share that view," Chan said dryly. "But what is the nature of the Scroll of Batu Khan that causes a scholar such as you such painful agitation? It has great value, perhaps?"

"Indeed it does!" C.V. Soong cried. "As you know, Mr. Chan, I have long been a scholar and collector of Oriental history. I have had in my possession for many years six priceless scrolls of Batu Khan and the Golden Horde. They are unique, irreplaceable, international treasures. The only authentic records of the Khanate of the Golden Horde!"

"I see," Chan said. "Great treasures, but who—?"

Lt. Forbes said, "I guess I'm ignorant, but what is the Golden Horde, and who was Batu Khan?"

"Who was—?" C.V. Soong slowly shook his head. "My apologies, Lieutenant, I forget that the young of America have so little interest in history or the Orient."

The older man paused, sighed, "I'm sure you

know that in the early 16th Century, the great Ghengis Khan led his Mongol horsemen out of the wastelands north of China to conquer most of the world of Asia, the Middle East, and eastern Europe. His method was not to use one army, but many armies under strong generals all at the same time, so that in the end his armies before and after his death became led by his sons and grandsons, and became dominant in different areas."

"One grandson," Chan explained, "the great Kublai Khan, became emperor of China, founder of the Yuan dynasty."

"The oldest grandson was Batu, and he led the invasions of Europe," C.V. Soong went on. "He conquered almost all of European Russia between 1235 and 1240, and probably could have taken all of Europe—he reached the Adriatic Sea and central Germany, defeated the Hungarians. But in 1241 Ghengis's successor as great Khan, Batu's uncle Ogadai, died, and Batu withdrew to Russia to be nearer the Mongol capital at Karakorum."

Chan said, "There is no doubt that European history was changed by Batu's withdrawal in 1241, as Russian history was made by his settling with his armies in Russia."

"He founded the Khanate of Kipchak, better known by its Russian name of the Golden Horde," C.V. Soong said. "The Khanate of the Golden Horde ruled most of Russia for two hundred years until broken up by Tamerlane, and even then the Crimean Khanate went on to almost 1800! A power that changed the world left as a record only six scrolls from its early days—three from Batu's own time, and three from his successor Berke Khan's time."

"And you own all six scrolls?" Forbes said.

Soong nodded, "Think of it—the only records of events that changed the destiny of Asia and Europe! I have written a book on them, lent them to museums, and had scholars from both Russia and China come to study them. Recently, I agreed to give them on a year's loan to the Temple of the Golden Horde here."

"What exactly *is* this Temple of the Golden Horde?" Chan asked.

"The only temple in America of a small cult that has existed since Batu Khan's day, believers in Mongol Shamanism," Soong said. "They have copies of the scrolls, of course, but a few months ago they asked me to lend them the originals for a year of study, and I agreed. Great documents should be used, not kept in some vault. Because I had been working with them, and to lessen the danger of loss or damage, I sent them one at a time over a period of a few months. All arrived safely, until now."

"Benny Chan was carrying a scroll when he died?" Chan said.

"And the Temple doesn't have it! The fifth scroll," Soong said. "I want—"

"Who would steal this scroll?" Chan broke in. "Such a unique document would be most difficult to realize a profit on."

"I can't imagine," Soong agreed. "Unless—"

Lieutenant Forbes walked to a large steel cabinet in the corner of his office. He opened the deep bottom drawer; and when he turned he held a large wooden chest, brass bound with a brass lock, about the size of a women's make-up case. "Is this your Golden Horde scroll, Mr. Soong?"

"Yes!" the philanthropist cried. "At least, it's the chest; the scroll was inside."

Soong hurried forward, fumbling in his pocket for his keys. Forbes shook his head and lifted the heavy lid of the chest.

"We had to pick the lock to see what was inside," Forbes said. "But we didn't damage the lock."

Chan said quickly, "It was locked when found?"

"Locked tight," Forbes said. "It's a strong lock, too."

Soong lifted out two cylinders of ancient vellum rolled around two polished wood sticks.

He opened the scroll, studied it for a moment. "It is the Batu Scroll, undamaged!"

"Where was it found, Lieutenant?" Chan asked.

"On the Temple grounds, on the beach about a half a mile from the road. It was in plain sight, and the spot was just about where Benny must have fallen in to be carried on the currents where we

33

found his body."

Chan looked at Soong. "Are you sure the scroll is genuine—the original?"

"Absolutely. See, my mark is on it."

Forbes said, "So much for that robbery motive, Inspector."

"It would seem so," Chan agreed. "Theft does not appear to be the cause of Benny Chan's accident."

"A great weight lifted," C.V. Soong said. "I must admit I was concerned that my scroll had caused the death of the man who carried it. A relief to know that was not so."

"All four previous scrolls were sent in the same manner?" Chan asked. "By simple messenger, all in the open?"

Soong nodded, "I did not want to risk loss in the mail or by parcel service, and the Temple sent the same handyman each time. They assured me that because of his mental handicap he was the most reliable messenger, would never let the chest out of his sight, would be extra careful. There was no previous trouble."

"Then you were not concerned by the possibility of theft?"

For an instant, the philanthropist seemed to hesitate. Then he shook his head, "No, I was not, not really. In any event, the handyman seemed a most inconspicuous carrier."

Chan nodded, and the philanthropist put the scroll back into its chest. He locked the chest and turned to the door.

"Will it now go to the Temple as arranged?" Chan said.

"I will take it there personally in the morning," C.V. Soong said. "Thank you for finding it, Lieutenant It is always a pleasure to meet you again, Inspector Chan."

"The honor is mine," Chan said.

C.V. Soong bowed and left the office. Chan seemed to watch the door thoughtfully as it closed behind the philanthropist. Lieutenant Forbes watched Chan.

"You're still not satisfied it was an accidental drowning, Inspector? What more do you need to know? Nothing was stolen from Benny Chan. If someone had been after that scroll, we wouldn't have found it right there on the beach."

"Unless Benny Chan was also carrying something unknown," Chan said. "Perhaps unknown even to Benny."

"Like what?" Forbes said. "And wouldn't the killer have taken the scroll then for a cover?"

"That would seem logical, yes," Chan mused. "A visit to the Temple is indicated. If the Lieutenant would direct me?"

Forbes gave the detective directions to the isolated temple, and Chan went out into the night to his car.

As he drove off, the night fog of the Northern California coast thickened over the wooded land.

* * *

The fog drifted around the high iron gates of the isolated estate on Half Moon Bay, and nothing moved in the chill night as Charlie Chan parked. He got out and, in the distance through the bars of the gate, he saw three buildings shrouded by trees. There was a small light in the structure nearest the ocean, but the other two were dark.

The large main gate was locked, but Chan soon found the side gate in the high fence. It was un-locked. It creaked open on rusted hinges, and Chan slipped through into the silent grounds. He stood for a time, listening, then began to walk silently up a curving gravel drive.

A half a mile in from the gate the first building loomed up through the night and fog—a silent, Chi-nese pagoda!

It was on a rise of ground facing the ocean a few hundred yards away. Wreathed in the night mist, its curved roof towered three stories high, and fierce dragon-heads snarled in silence from the curved-up corners of its high roof. Dark pillars rose from the open porch to support the roof. There were no win-dows.

A circular, latticed gate guarded the entry por-tal. It wasn't locked, and Chan pushed it open and entered the dark gloom of the interior. Sweet, thick incense greeted him, and as his eyes became accustomed to the dark inside, he saw a tall, bare altar that had been carved from a single giant boulder. It stood at the very rear of the high room and still retained its natural shape. A row of tiny candles burned on either side, set in deep, dark blue containers and almost invisible—moving only faintly like the wind itself.

A live tree grew from a patch of bare earth behind the stone altar up through an opening in the ceiling, and paintings of harsh mountains stood on each side of the tree. Above it all was a vaulted dome painted a sky blue with painted white clouds, a painted representation of Genghis Khan, and a single word—*Tengri*. Chan stared up at the strange altar and painted sky and spoke softly to himself:

"*Tengri*, the blue sky of Genghis Khan."

The rest of the large room was unfurnished, without seats of any kind. Magical circles had been painted on the bare wood floor as if the worshippers sat in circular groups. More magical symbols were drawn on all the walls, and two shaman costumes hung near the stone altar, costumes not very different from those of native American medicine men.

A shamanist temple, for worshipers of the sky, mountains, rocks, forest and wind. The "spirits" present in these powers of nature could be contacted only by the magic of the shaman, the intercessor between the spirits of nature and the people. An ancient religion, primitive and out of place in the modern world, and yet, as Chan stood alone in the dark temple, he seemed to feel the powers of nature, hear the howl of the forest wind.

Wind somewhere that was almost a scream.

A demon of the wind, and a scream . . .

A real scream!

No wind, no demon had voiced that cry, Chan realized suddenly. It had been a human, and close by.

Chan turned and hurried toward the round entry portal. The scream came again, somewhere out in the night . . . no, not a scream, exactly, but more a wild shriek of terror. A series of terrified cries, wild and almost hysterical, frantic and moving, out there in the night as if someone fled from a mortal danger.

Chan was halfway from the altar to the entry portal when the almost-animal cries echoed inside the temple itself. Chan stopped.

V

THE GIRL stood just inside the entry portal, her burning eyes searching wildly from side to side, her cries now low moans of fear. A tall, thin girl in her early twenties, pretty, with long blonde hair, a sensual mouth, and wide brown eyes. Manic eyes, hysterical, half-insane. She wore a long, flowing white Oriental robe, but she was caucasian. By the dim light of the candles, Chan saw that the white robe was stained with dirt and grass.

Chan stepped forward, "Don't be afraid, Miss—"

"Ahhhh—!" The girl shrank back against a wall, her thin body trembling violently, her eyes staring crazily.

"Please, I will not harm—"

Chan saw the knife then. A long, thin dagger with a red-jeweled handle and a needle-sharp ten-inch blade. The girl held it out in front of her.

With a cry, she leaped toward the detective, the knife held high and aimed at his heart.

Startled, Chan stepped backward. His rear foot slipped on the bare wood floor, and he fell. The girl was on him, the dagger plunging straight down at his chest!

Chan, all his muscles trained by years of T'ai-Chi-Chuan, caught her wrist and rolled aside in one fluid movement. The Chinese system of physical fitness and self-defense had kept him powerful and supple beyond his years, and the violent girl was helpless in his grip. The dagger fell to the floor. Chan rose swiftly to his feet, still grasping the girl's wrist.

"Stand still," he said sharply. The tall girl glared at him, breathing hard from the fight. Her face was as pale as her white robe, and her dilated eyes rolled in her head like dark marbles floating in liquid. Chan studied her. There was hysteria in her eyes, and terror. The detective made his voice gentle to soothe and calm her:

"Of what are you so frightened, my child?"

The girl whimpered, and her lips parted—but the voice that spoke wasn't hers!

A deep, masculine voice from the entry portal to the dark temple said, "She is a sick girl, afraid of herself."

Chan loooked up to see a tall, elegant man in a gray tweed business suit. He came into the temple carrying a flashlight and talking to the girl, "The shadows won't hurt you, Angela. Nothing is going to hurt you. I've come to help."

His handsome face was tanned, his dark hair flecked with gray, and his suit custom made. He had an aura of authority, and his sharp brown eyes were angry under their calm surface. He, too, was breathing hard as if he'd been running. Chan watched him as he went on calming the girl, speaking to her in a soft, hypnotic voice.

"The fear of shadows," Chan said, "can be lethal when accompanied by a dagger in the hand." He held up the knife he had taken from the girl.

The tall man glared. "Her fears are our concern," he said. "What the devil are you doing here, and who are you?"

"I'm here to speak with the Khan of the Temple on the matter of Benny Chan's accident," Chan said quietly. "My name is also Chan, Inspector of the Honolulu Police Department."

The tall man seemed to hesitate. "Chan? You're a relative of poor Benny's?"

"Perhaps distant—all Chans are of one ancient family—but I did not know the drowned man. I am here as a policeman and not as a relation."

A sudden wariness came over the tall man. He tried to hide it, but it was there. He glanced at the girl. Chan saw that she was now staring at him, an odd light in her manic eyes, a hint of purpose under the hysteria that shook her.

The tall man spoke quietly, his voice controlled: "A Honolulu policeman? Why would the Honolulu police be concerned with an accident here?"

"Benny Chan's sister asked that I give some small assistance to the local police."

"But Benny's death was a simple accident. The police confirmed that."

"Undoubtedly true," Chan said with a faint smile. "All that remains is to remove sisterly doubts. I am certain the Khan of this Temple can do that, and perhaps yourself, Mr.—?"

"Well—" the tall man began and frowned. "Of course, Inspector, we'll help all we can. I'm Carleton Sedgwick, lawyer for the Temple. I conduct all outside business, but I really don't see what more I can do for the police that I haven't already done. Poor Benny was simply returning from an errand and must have lost his way in the fog and fallen into the ocean. He wasn't very bright, you know."

"The retarded have some difficulty with the large world," Chan observed, "but usually they become most familiar with the small world where they live. Like blind men, retarded people are more careful than normal people, stay with what they know. It is odd that he lost his way on the grounds he called home."

Carleton Sedgwick nodded. "True, Inspector, but Benny was easily panicked. He was late in coming home that night, it was dark and foggy, and perhaps some innocent occurrence frightened him and he simply lost his head."

"Sounds very logical," Chan agreed. "Perhaps you are aware of some such occurrence that night? Saw or heard something?"

"I'm afraid not. I wasn't here, and the Khan and Princess were in their residence. None of us knew Benny had returned. In fact, we became worried by morning and called the police. Benny was carrying a priceless ancient scroll, and we found his pickup truck sitting outside the gate."

"And Benny Chan was found at last in the ocean," Chan said.

"Tragic," Sedgwick said.

Chan nodded thoughtfully. "You have been a lawyer for the Temple long, Mr. Sedgwick? Do they have much need for a lawyer?"

"I've been their lawyer for six years, and I'm afraid they do need a lawyer often. People do not always like other cultures' rites, Inspector. They become angry or scared by what they don't understand, and they try to shut us down or worse. Then I go to work."

Chan nodded and looked at the now silent girl. "This young woman is a member of the Temple?"

"In a way, Inspector. A candidate for inclusion," Sedgwick said. "We have what other religions would call a 'Retreat House.' A place of therapy for those disturbed by the chaos of the outside world. A sanctuary for contemplation and solace, peace and understanding, for exorcism of the hidden evils inside."

"You are, then, psychiatrists?"

"No, certainly not!" Sedgwick snapped. "That would be illegal, and you know it. The Khan only instructs in ancient methods of self-control, of contemplation, of the peace that comes with oneness with the universe. He initiates the sufferers in the Rites of the Golden Horde to exorcise their private demons."

"You yourself are a believer, Mr. Sedgwick?"

"I'm afraid it isn't my calling," the lawyer said stiffly. "But I have seen the Khan do fine work with those who need aid."

"The process is not yet effective with this young woman," Chan said dryly. "Or perhaps some event has caused a sudden relapse?"

"Nothing has—" Sedgwick began.

The scream that echoed through the temple was half moan, half cry of terror—half fear and half anguish. Angela had never taken her eyes from Chan all the time he had been talking to Carleton Sedgwick, and now her scream flowed through the dark temple like something alive.

"Please, what is wrong, Angela?" Chan asked.

Her eyes never moved, staring at Chan and at the same time staring at something unseen beyond him, and her mouth open and screaming by itself unconnected to her eyes.

"The scroll!" the girl cried, moaning in horror, raising her arm as if to protect herself. "It's sacred! The scroll, violated! *Unclean!* I saw him! He violated the sacred scroll! *Pursued!* They have come for him! The demons!"

Her scream rose again, shattering the night, "*The demons!* I see them! Oh . . . Oh . . . *Don't touch me!* . . . don't . . ."

Chan's dark eyes narrowed. "Who do the demons pursue?"

"I see them! *Don't let them touch me!*" Angela cried.

Chan kept his grip on her arm; she twisted and thrashed as if slimy things crawled all over her, and her dilated eyes were enormous in the dim temple. Something about her—drugged? Her brain disturbed, a bad trip, seeing demons?

"Tell me," Chan urged, "what do you see? Where?"

Her head swung back and forth, thrashing. "No faces! They have no faces! Oh, God, the scroll has been violated! Oh—"

Sedgwick was pale. "Angela! Stop! There are no—"

"*Ahhhhhhhhhh!*" the girl screamed. It was an animal cry, torn from somewhere deep inside her frail body.

The cry—and then she broke free and ran! Ran

for the freedom of the outdoors. Suddenly, before Chan or Carleton Sedgwick could move, Angela Smith was at the portal.

"Quick!" Chan hissed. "After her!"

But the girl had stopped. Something strange now moved in the shadows outside.

Chan watched as an otherworldly figure came forward into the temple, an apparition in the skin of some wild animal. It had the head of a great, horned yak, the tail of a snow tiger, and long streamers of horsehair hanging from its spread arms. A tall staff in one paw hung with the tails of small beasts, and a rattle in the other paw whirred as the apparition swung it rapidly in a circle like some aboriginal bull-roarer.

Its mouth opened, and a sound came out like the wind sweeping across a vast, bare plain.

Angela Smith stared, suddenly calm, trans-fixed.

VI

THE APPARITION flung its arms wide. "Spirits come free!" it cried in a deep, clear voice. The words were in English. "Spirit of the wind! Spirit of the forest! Spirit of the river! Spirit of the blue sky! Enter this child of the great Khan!"

Angela Smith stood immobile, her pale face turned up to the painted sky of the macabre temple, her whole body now quiet, calm. The apparition—the shaman, Chan assumed—waved his staff, whirled his rattle, and cried out again. The same words, but in some other language now. A language Chan recognized as Mongolian.

And once more in Mongolian and then again in English—"Oh spirits of the land enter and destroy the demons of the dark! Ride down the wind and sky, trample the evil demons with the thunder of your pony's hooves! Strike them with your sword! Bring the clear blue sky of the great Khan into her body! Release her! Show us a sign of your power!"

Arms high, the shaman then uttered Mongolian words Chan didn't know. Magical words, their meanings lost long ago in the sands of history and time. Magical incantations, repeated over and over.

A change came over Angela Smith.

Color crept into her pale face. Her eyes cleared, brightened. Her young lips moved in a silent incantation of her own, and then, slowly, her whole tall body went limp. She sank to her knees with her eyes turned up toward the sky of the dark temple.

She knelt there, calm, breathing easily now, and then her clear eyes turned to the shaman with something that Chan saw was close to love. If not sensual love, then devotion, trust, a deep and quiet peace.

"Now you will rest, child," the shaman said.

Carleton Sedgwick said, "Remarkable, Li! A great power is in you, a power for good."

"No," the shaman said quietly in English now, "the power is in her, in the belief. I am only the instrument through which the believer recognizes his own peace and good."

Then the weird apparition of the shaman reached up and removed the horned yak head, revealing the small, thin face of a Chinese man in his mid-fifties. A deeply lined face, clean-shaven, with burning black eyes that were amazingly gentle despite the obvious fire in them, that turned toward Chan.

"Who is our guest, Carleton?"

Sedgwick nodded to Chan, "He says his name is Chan, a detective from Honolulu. Inspector, this is Li Po, the Khan of the Temple of the Golden Horde."

"Honored," Chan said with a small bow.

The Khan, Li Po, frowned and then suddenly smiled. "Chan? The famous Charlie Chan? It is Li Po who is honored. Our small temple rejoices in such an eminent presence!"

"Fame is a thing of the mist," Chan said. "Your power to exorcise demons of troubled minds is greater than my fleeting honors."

Before Khan Li Po could reply again, there was a liquid, sibilant sound at the portal of the temple. A swishing like some great bird in the night, and a small woman in voluminous, brocaded silk robes seemed to sweep into the temple.

"He must go, Khan! He violates the temple!"

She was a tiny woman, Oriental but not Chinese, with a low, cultured voice. In her early forties, her small, beautiful face was as unlined as the face of a child. Under the stiff robe her tiny body was as slim as a girl. But her almond eyes were not the eyes of a child or of a girl. There was something powerful and imposing about her tiny figure.

"A stranger," she cried. "He pollutes the Temple!"

Chan said, "Are not all men brothers under the

blue sky of the great Kahn, Tengri?"

"It is true, Princess," the Khan said. "Tengri is for all."

The Khan's voice had a trance-like gentleness like something from another world. Chan studied the thin leader of the Temple from under hooded eyes. Was the man under some kind of drug? It wasn't unusual for cults to use drugs to heighten their senses, or to tranquilize members into a state of euphoria.

Carleton Sedgwick was also watching the Khan, though trying not to show he was. The tall lawyer had stepped closer to the small, fiery woman who also watched the shaman. Chan had the sudden sensation that the lawyer and the tiny woman were a team, joined together. The woman herself was glaring at the Khan, her tiny foot tapping in a kind of anger.

The Khan, Li Po, seemed to hear the tapping of the woman's foot, and his eyes blinked. He came out of the trance-like state. He nodded to Chan.

"Humble apologies, Inspector Chan, I fail to introduce my wife, this lady before you. I present Madame Li, Snow Princess of the Golden Horde."

Chan bowed to cover his surprise. The tiny woman was the wife of the Khan, and yet. . . ? Had Chan's impression that Madame Li and Sedgwick were, somehow, a team been erroneous? No, he didn't think so. There was something between the tiny woman and the lawyer, something shared, but perhaps, only for the moment. Something about the girl, Angela Smith? He hid behind a smile.

"Such beauty is met with only a few times in a long life," he said.

"Flattery undeserved, but pleasing," Madame Li said. She smiled, bowed, and then looked boldly at Chan. "Yet I must say again that we cannot allow outsiders to invade our peace. You bring alien spirits, Inspector Chan, to disturb our peace."

"Peace is to be prized," Chan said softly, "yet, somehow, peace seems to elude young Angela Smith. She is troubled."

Madame Li shook her tiny head. "Angela has been with us but a short time. Inner peace is not bought quickly in a discount shop. Truth is slow, like the cleaning action of the wind and rain."

She glanced toward the tall girl, who was still on her knees, calm now, and still looking at the Khan with that sense of love, of total trust, of a kind of sensuality. Madame Li stepped to her, touched her shoulder.

"She came to us very sick, and we have helped her along the path of recovery," the tiny Princess said, "but she has far to travel, is still confused, and must not be disturbed."

Carleton Sedgwick said, "She has hallucinations, Inspector; sees visions that scare the hell out of her. That's what happened tonight. She had a spell, escaped from the sanctuary house, and I was chasing her when she attacked you."

"Now she must rest," Madame Li said. "Come, child. Return to the peace of the sanctuary."

The woman bent to raise the kneeling girl. For an instant, Angela seemed to resist, her eyes fixed only on the Khan. She trembled, shrank away, and her high voice was shaking:

"The . . . demons . . . I saw the . . . demons. . . ."

The Khan nodded, smiled gently, "But they are gone, the demons. You are safe, you are one with the Golden Horde. You must return to the oneness of our love. Go now, my child."

"One," she said. "Yes. Peace."

She stood, smiling now, and seemed to walk in a trance, inside a glass bubble, toward the Temple portal. Madame Li was beside her, and Sedgwick just behind her. The Khan and Chan came last. They all walked across the dark, misty grounds to the largest of the two ordinary buildings. It was a square building of yellow stucco, two stories high, with all its windows barred. There was light on the first floor.

Inside, the lobby looked like a hospital or rest home lobby. Madame Li turned the tall girl over to a burly man and a big, heavy woman, both wearing kimonos decorated with some of the same magical symbols from the Temple. They escorted the girl through a barred and locked gate, then down a corridor.

"We will go to my office, Inspector Chan," The Khan said.

The Khan led Chan outside, and together with Madame Li and Sedgwick, they crossed under the dark trees to the third building. Smaller, it was also yellow stucco, two stories high, but without bars on the windows. The Khan's office was more like a small chapel, lit by flickering candles and full of the smell of some clean, forest-like incense. There were no chairs or couches, nothing but thick rugs and cushions on the floor, and a low Japanese-style desk a few inches high. The Khan sat cross-legged behind his desk, and waved Chan to sit facing him on a cushion in the same Oriental manner. Madame Li and Sedgwick reclined on cushions across the dim room. Sedgwick did not seem comfortable, his long legs unaccustomed to sitting Oriental fashion.

"So," the Khan said, smiling sadly, "you have come, of course, to speak of Benny, of his accident. It weighs on us all, a thing difficult to understand. I have communed with the spirits, but as yet they have given no answer."

"You do not think it was an accident?" Chan said quickly.

"In Western eyes, perhaps it was what you call an accident. But to us, Inspector, there are no accidents. All is in the realm of the spirits, all is the will of some spirit. It is for us to try to understand the will of the spirits, to accept the event."

"The girl, Angela Smith, spoke of demons pursuing one who had violated the sacred scroll carried by Benny Chan. Perhaps she has seen something? Or saw Benny Chan do something?"

Madame Li snapped, "Angela is lost in visions out of time!"

"Hallucinations, Mr. Chan," Carleton Sedgwick said. "Maybe Benny's accident set her off, scared her, or gave her nightmares."

"A deluded girl frightened by the accident?" Chan said.

"That's it," Sedgwick agreed.

"No!" the Khan said suddenly. They all looked at the thin shaman. His eyes burned. "The demons are real, Inspector. They are demon spirits of evil! Angela saw real demons!" The Khan's eyes seemed to glow in the flickering candlelight. "There are no accidents, and Angela saw demons. I know that; it is my calling to know," the thin, intense man said. "She has been granted a vision of the demons who caused Benny to die."

"A vision?" Chan said, frowned at the Khan. "I am confused, Mr. Li. Did Angela Smith see demons pursue Benny Chan, or did she only have a vision of seeing demons?"

"There is no difference," the Khan said. "Demons do not live as we, do not have time and space as we. To see demons in a vision of sleep is the same as seeing demons awake in the night."

"Was she there when Benny fell into the ocean?"

"She was there, and she was in her room. If she saw the demons, she was there no matter where she was in flesh."

Madame Li said, "He does not understand our faith, great Khan. For him, Angela saw or dreamed." She looked at Chan. "For the Khan, Mr. Chan, flesh and spirit are one. A vision, a dream, a hallucination are all as real as touch. But in your terms, no. Angela was not there, and there are no demons."

"There are demons," the Khan said, "and they pursued poor Benny. How else would a man who feared water drown? It was known that Benny would not go near water; only a demon could have made him go where he could drown. That is truth!"

Carleton Sedgwick laughed; "It's not a truth an American cop is going to believe. They don't arrest visions. Not that I ever heard."

"Yet it is the truth," the Khan said quietly. His deep eyes looked now at Chan. "Around all things of this world are the spirits of good and evil. Around great things are very strong spirits. Benny Chan carried from Honolulu the sacred scroll of Batu Khan, and its spirits and demons came with it. You know of the sacred scrolls of the Golden Horde, Inspector Chan?"

"Some knowledge," Chan said.

The thin, intense man seemed lost in a trance in the dim, incensed room. "The scrolls are sacred to us; we have lived by their words of contemplation and love, the words of soldiers who had come through the fires of violence to peace. But we have had only copies. A scholar in Hawaii, a benefactor, agreed to lend us the originals. Four came to us, carried by Benny Chan. The fifth was on its way when Benny disappeared."

The Khan shook his head sadly. "They are powerful things, the scrolls, with powerful spirits—and powerful demons. The demons wish to keep the scrolls from our Temple, so they destroyed Benny Chan. But he was true to his trust, and the scroll was not destroyed. Soon, we will have it."

The Khan finished and fell silent. No one spoke.

"They are valuable, the scrolls?" Chan said at last.

But the Khan didn't answer. He sat on his cushion behind the low desk and slowly began to rock back and forth. His mouth opened and he began to chant some slow song in Mongol words. Madame Li spoke from the corner.

"He cannot hear you now, Inspector. He is in his trance, at his devotions. But I will answer. The value of the scrolls is beyond price—and it is also nothing at all. No one could sell the scrolls because none would buy them. Each scroll is unique, known

56

to every scholar of Russian or Chinese history."

"There are those who steal for other rewards than money," Chan said. "Simply to own what is unique."

"But no one tried to steal the scroll," Carleton Sedgwick said. "The police found it where poor Benny dropped it. If someone wanted to steal the scroll, they wouldn't have left it on the beach."

"It would not seem so," Chan agreed, watching Madame Li and Sedgwick. "Death of Benny Chan appear not caused by valuable scroll. Yet I have observed a sudden interest in Benny's sister and in myself after contact by his sister."

"Interest, Mr. Chan?" Madame Li said. "What interest do you mean?"

"Men follow both Benny's sister and myself in San Francisco. Men who try very hard to remain unknown and unseen."

Chan spoke casually, but his hooded eyes had been watching Madame Li and Sedgwick the whole time. For a split second, the lawyer seemed startled. A flash of reaction, no more, and gone just as quickly. Madame Li sat impassive.

"You have no knowledge of who these men could be?" the tiny Snow Princess said.

"Not at the moment," Chan admitted. "Is it possible that you would know some explanation?"

"No, Inspector, we do not," Madame Li said.

"Unless they're some more of Li Po's demons,"

Sedgwick said.

Chan smiled. "Ah, perhaps so. Perhaps the same imaginary demons seen by Angela Smith, and the same demons that forced a man afraid of water to drown."

"There are forces and shadows on this earth we mortals do not know, Mr. Chan," Madame Li said.

"But also forces and shadows known only too well—forces of fear and greed," Chan said quietly. He stood and bowed briefly. "I will not disturb you further tonight."

He turned and left the dim, candlelit room with its heavy atmosphere of incense. The Khan had not moved an inch since he had last spoken, except to rock gently from side to side like a tree in the gentle wind. Madame Li sat equally impassive, her sharp eyes following Chan as he left. Only Carleton Sedgwick moved, seemed to lick his lips, nervous.

Outside, Chan walked back down the gravel drive in the dark night. As he walked, he thought about the Temple of the Golden Horde. One thing was clear to him; the Khan believed in the truth of his Temple, and perhaps Madame Li did also, but Carleton Sedgwick was no believer in spirits or demons or temples.

VII

THE WINTER DAWN of the next morning was clear in San Francisco. The city came awake slowly, the streets starting to move as the first early-morning people emerged from the old frame houses on the steep hills that bordered the great bay.

Charlie Chan, the windows of his suite wide open to admit the clear dawn air, sat immobile and silent in the lotus position. He had been in this position of contemplation since dawn.

He breathed deeply and without any visible effort.

At precisely half an hour after dawn, he moved, rose, and began his daily ten-minute exercise of the ancient Chinese discipline of T'ai-Chi-Chuan. The system of ballet-like calisthenics for physical fitness and self-defense was an art of balance and grace without overt strength, and in the hands of a lifetime practitioner like Chan, it gave a skill absolutely deadly in effect.

His ten minutes over, the detective showered, dressed, and sat for a time in thought. Only his veiled black eyes moved as he concentrated on his thoughts. At last he stood and went to the telephone. He placed a long-distance call to Honolulu and instructed his office to make a complete check of the activities of Benny Chan in Hawaii.

He then made a local call to the San Francisco Police and his old friend Captain Mort Wade.

"Charlie!" Captain Wade cried. "It's good to hear from you! I'm sorry I missed your talk yesterday, but I was on duty."

"I had hoped to call for a social visit with my old friend when all the speechmaking was concluded."

"Just name the time, Charlie," Wade said at once.

"I'm afraid it must wait a few days. This call is prompted by business, not pleasure. You know of a cult named Temple of the Golden Horde?"

"I've heard of it," Wade said. "Somewhere down the peninsula near Half Moon Bay, isn't it? A legitimate operation as far as I've heard. Why?"

Chan explained about Benny Chan, and the doubts of Betty Chan. "I'd like to learn more of the background of Li Po who is Khan of cult, and of his wife, Madame Li. And I need to know the same for lawyer named Carleton Sedgwick."

"I'll get someone on it right away. Anything, else?"

"Yes, some background on Betty Chan, daughter of Chan Wu Han, once waiter at Kung Shi Restaurant. She lives in Chinatown," and he gave the girl's address.

"Okay, Charlie, and don't forget that social visit."

"The pleasure will be mine."

Chan's third call was to Betty Chan. There was no answer. This made him frown. It was too early for the girl to be at work. He looked at his watch, and stood up. It was time for breakfast. As he walked to his door, there was a heavy knocking.

"Mr. Chan? It's C.V. Soong. I have to speak to you!"

Chan hesitated a second, found his pistol and slipped it into his pocket, and then opened the door. The tall, bone-thin old philanthropist hurried into the suite, motioning for Chan to close the door quickly.

His dignified face with its long white mustache was agitated. He wore western dress now, a gray suit, blue shirt, and tie, and seemed suddenly much older. He carried the heavy, brass-bound box of the sacred scroll.

"I think I'm being watched, Inspector! Followed!"

Chan's eyes narrowed. "Can you describe your suspected watchers?"

Soong described two men, one of them much like the man Chan had seen following himself!

"You know these men?" Chan asked.

"I . . . I'm not sure, Inspector," the old man said. "It's possible I've seen one of them before—in Honolulu! Some time ago, perhaps six months. Near my house."

"At about the time you decided to present scrolls for loan to Temple of the Golden Horde?"

Soong nodded. "Yes, just about then! But I have no idea who they could be. Only—" The old man bit his lip, looked around nervously, and then sat down on a couch. He was pale as he looked up at Chan.

"I was about to take the scroll down to Li Po at the Temple, but now I'm afraid. Perhaps someone does want to steal it!"

"For what reason, Mr. Soong? All agree that the scroll is unique, could not be sold."

"I know, and the greatest value of the scrolls is largely for scholars, for study. Even an eccentric collector would get little pleasure if he couldn't show them. But—" the old man hesitated again, went on chewing his lip nervously. "It would be of great value in two places, Mr. Chan, where it could be shown without any danger of arrest by American authorities. Two places where it could be wanted very much, and shown publicly in defiance of being returned—by the governments of Communist China and Soviet Russia!"

"They would want the scrolls?"

"They have for a long time, since the scrolls are part of the history of both nations. Their scholars have made many offers, but I have always refused. The scrolls would be of immense national value to both countries."

Chan considered for a time. The men he had seen tailing him and Betty Chan, and now C.V. Soong, could be professional agents.

"Yet," Chan said slowly, "if agents are attempting to steal the scrolls, why was the fifth scroll found abandoned on a beach?"

"I don't know. Perhaps Benny Chan dropped it in the fog, and the agents were scared away by something before they could find it that night."

"Perhaps so," Chan said, and he thought about Angela Smith and her vision of seeing demons.

"Mr. Chan, I'm scared," C.V. Soong said. "Would you take the scroll to the Temple? In your hands I know it would be safely delivered."

"If agents of China or Russia want the scrolls, would they not attempt to steal all of them from the Temple?" Chan asked.

"The Khan has them locked up well. I made sure he had strong security."

Chan rubbed his chin. "It's odd that only the fifth scroll would be target of theft and possible murder. What is special about this scroll? What changed on this trip of Benny Chan from Hawaii?"

"Nothing that I know of, but . . . Please, Inspector. I am too old to risk agents attacking me."

"Very well. I will deliver the scroll."

"Thank you!" Soong said fervently. "I'll see that you are well paid for your trouble."

"Pay is not required. Perhaps you will donate to some charity in my name."

"Of course," the old man agreed, and stood up. He smiled now. "I am most grateful, Inspector."

Chan nodded, and the old man left the suite. After Soong had gone, Chan opened the heavy chest and looked again at the priceless scroll. He examined the heavy vellum and the polished wood spindles it was rolled on. There was nothing unusual about either. He opened the scroll and read the ancient writing. It was slow work, since Chan knew only a little ancient Mongolian, but the words seemed to be what they were supposed to be.

He closed the box and went to the telephone again. Once more he dialed Betty Chan's number. There was still no answer. A trace of worry appeared on his smooth, ivory face. He got his black overcoat, picked up the box, and went out. He rode down to the lobby in the elevator and had the scroll placed in the hotel safe.

Then he went out into the cold sun and hailed a taxi.

VIII

BETTY CHAN lived in an old, three-story walk-up apartment on a narrow Chinatown street near the edge of North Beach on one of the old Barbary Coast hills. Chan stood in a shadowed doorway across from the building and silently watched.

In the morning hours the street busy with traffic and thronged with hardworking Chinese-Americans hurrying to their destinations. Chan waited quietly, looking for signs of the men who had been following Betty Chan, C.V. Soong, and himself. He didn't see any of them. The only people lounging on the crowded street, not hurrying past, were three Chinese youths in modern-American long hair and jeans and black leather jackets.

Chan noted these youths with a small sigh— the new ways of youth had reached even into the close-knit society of Chinatown. Chan neither approved nor objected to the new youth, he was only a little sad to see the traditional ways fading. It was inevitable; time and distance changed all, and an intelligent man did not oppose the inevitable, but a man could regret the loss of identity. The great culture of China had . . .

Chan saw the curtain move at a high window in Betty Chan's building. A quick movement, furtive, and it was the window of what had to be Betty Chan's own apartment!

Someone was in the girl's rooms, and there had been no answer to his telephone calls.

Still Chan watched.

The movement of the curtain came again!

Someone was looking down at the street. Chan tried the door behind him, which led into an apartment building. It was open. He went through and along the corridor to the rear entrance. It opened out into one of the narrow back alleys of Chinatown, cluttered with trash cans and the high fire escapes.

Turning, he went along the alley to the cross street, walked back to the corner and across the street so he couldn't been seen from Betty Chan's window. He glided along in the shadow of the buildings to her entrance. No one seemed to be watching him; even the long-haired Chinese youth were gone now. He slipped through the door and into her building.

It was dim inside, the stairs up narrow and

dirty. Nothing seemed to move in the corridors. Chan went up as silent as a ghost. On the landing below the girl's top-floor apartment, he stopped and listened. He heard nothing above. He went on up even more slowly.

There was a faint sound behind the closed door of Betty Chan's apartment. A soft sound like someone stepping quietly.

Chan drew his small pistol. Barely breathing, he listened, and the sound came again—someone was walking very lightly inside the apartment as if on eggshells.

Chan saw a ladder at the end of the hall, which had to lead to the roof. He climbed up, pushed open the trap, and emerged onto a flatsunlit roof. The fire escape on this building was in the front. He had seen that from below. He descended the iron rungs cautiously, then crouched with his pistol ready outside Betty Chan's bedroom window. This was not the window where he had seen the curtain move. Peeking inside, he took in a small bedroom, spotlessly neat and empty of people. The door into the next room closed. Raising the window slowly and silently, Chan climbed inside and paused, listening. Then he saw Betty Chan's handbag and coat on the chair!

He stared at the handbag and coat for a time—what woman went out without her handbag? Or her coat on a day as cool as this one?

A floorboard in the next room creaked. Chan looked at the closed door. Where was Betty Chan, and who was walking so softly out in the girl's living room?

The detective eased the safety off on his pistol, stepped close to the door, and listened again. He heard the clink of something—metal against glass or china.

Chan took a breath and flung the door open in a sweeping movement, jumping out into the living room with amazing agility for a man of his age and portliness.

"Do not move, please!" Chan commanded.

Betty Chan's scream echoed through the small living room. Her cup crashed to the floor, and she fainted, sprawling the the doorway to her kitchenette.

There was no one else in the small apartment. Betty Chan had been alone.

Surprised, Chan hurried to her. He got some water from the sink and gently revived her. She stared up at him still with terror on her face.

"It is all right," Chan smiled. "Only Inspector Chan."

"I . . . I thought . . . you—"

Chan nodded. "Naturally you assumed I was an intruder. I entered in so unfortunate a manner because my repeated telephone calls received no answer."

"It's not your fault, Inspector," Betty Chan said.

The girl got up by herself and, trembling, sat in the nearest chair. She lit a cigarette, and her hands shook as she smoked. She gazed up at Chan.

"I was frightened," she said nervously. "That's why I didn't answer my telephone this morning." She looked at Chan with her eyes wide and scared. "Inspector, someone's been watching me! Early this morning someone tried to enter my apartment! I bolted the door, pushed a chair against it, and screamed, and he ran away! But I've seen them outside, watching! I know it!"

"I'm not surprised, Betty," Chan said. "Yesterday, when you left my hotel, I observed men following you. Later, a man followed me."

"Is that what you tried to call to tell me?"

Chan nodded.

The girl seemed to shudder. "Who could they be, and what do they want?" she said. "You think they might have . . . killed Benny?"

"Possibly. It's also possible they are agents of a foreign government and their purpose is to steal the valuable scroll Benny carried."

"But the scroll wasn't stolen, was it?"

"Perhaps Benny fooled them," Chan said.

"He would, you know! He was awful loyal to that Khan man, and he loved his job at the Temple," Betty said sadly, and then she shook her head. "Only, the men I saw watching me outside sure didn't look like foreign agents, Mr. Chan. They looked like thugs, you know, weird people all covered up in capes and big hats so I could hardly even see a face. Just standing down in the street last night late, not even hiding."

"Capes and hats? You are sure? They weren't men in very ordinary suits? One tall and wearing a brown suit? Carrying, perhaps, newspapers? Very casual?"

"Oh no, nothing at all like that, Inspector. These men were really weird . . . scary . . . and they acted like they wanted me to see them. The one who tried to break in made almost no sound when he ran away, like he was wearing sneakers."

Chan sat down slowly, facing the young woman. His veiled eyes were points like dark stone. He seemed to be lost in thought for some minutes as he watched Betty Chan.

"You have never seen these men before?"

"No. I . . . They scared me, and I think they wanted to."

"Betty, think very deeply. When Benny returned from Hawaii, did he contact you? Did he, possibly, call you from Hawaii? Did anything happen that was unusual? Anything to indicate that Benny had done anything, or was frightened of anyone?"

"I never saw him, Mr. Chan, not since the day before he left for Honolulu this time. He was happy . Doing an important job always made him feel useful. He must have gone directly from the airport to the Temple that night."

"No, the people at the Temple say he was late. They had expected him to return earlier. What would make him late?"

"I don't know. He didn't have any friends outside of me and at the Temple."

"He was somewhere," Chan said. "Time is missing. You are sure nothing strange happened, nothing—"

Betty Chan blinked. "Well . . . There was one little thing, Inspector, now that I think. I'd forgotten all about it. It didn't seem important, just very ordinary, and when Benny was found I forgot it."

"And you remember it now?"

"Well, it was just that I was out a little late that evening, didn't get home until about nine P.M. As I came in, my telephone was ringing. It stopped before I could get to it. I couldn't think of anyone it could have been except Benny!"

"He called you often?"

"Yes—especially if he had troubles. My number is unlisted, so it had to be someone I knew—or a wrong number, I guess."

"Wrong number is possible," Chan agreed thoughtfully. "Also, it is possible that your brother with a problem tried to call."

"Maybe if I'd been home—?" she trailed off, her face miserable as she thought of her dead brother trying to call her for help.

"I'm sure it could not have changed events," Chan said, and he stood up. "But events happen, and now I suggest you remain off the streets as much as possible."

"I've got to work, Mr. Chan. I can't hide."

"You work where?"

"At the Kung Fu Tze Book Store. Today is my day off."

Chan nodded. "Work and life must continue, and probably you are in no danger. But walk with care. If you see those men watching you again, seek safety and call me or the police."

"I will," Betty Chan said. "What are you going to do?"

"Deliver a valuable scroll to the Temple of Golden Horde," Chan said and smiled. "An opportunity, also, to pay a second visit to the Temple in the innocent guise of volunteer messenger."

"You suspect something at the Temple?"

"I am still very curious. A sick girl at the Temple may have seen more than she has yet told about the night your brother drowned. Some shadows appear to hang over the Temple. It may be something or nothing."

The eminent detective smiled kindly, nodded, and left the neat little apartment. On his way down the narrow stairs, he suddenly stopped. Had a door just ahead been open an inch or two? Open—and closed quietly as Chan appeared coming down? He wasn't sure.

He went on down, opened then closed the outer door without going through, and waited. He stood five minutes, but nothing happened in the silent building.

On the crowded street, as he caught a taxi to return to his hotel, he saw nothing suspicious. Only the hurrying throngs of the great city, the thousands of faces that could hide an equal number of secrets.

IX

A MESSAGE had been waiting for Charlie Chan at the hotel to call his office in Honolulu. He had done so, and as he drove once more down the peninsula in his rented Toyota, he considered the report of his staff.

Benny Chan had done absolutely nothing unusual in Hawaii. The handyman had arrived exactly as he had four times before, had gone directly to the house of C.V. Soong in one of the most exclusive sections of Honolulu, and had left the same day, carrying a box exactly like the other four he had carried previously. He had stopped nowhere, met no one, encountered nothing out of the usual.

Chan's drove took him to the high iron gates of the isolated Temple of the Golden Horde. In the sunlight, the eerie atmosphere that hung over the strange buildings in the fog of night was gone. It was only a green, pleasant country estate where the tall Chinese pagoda was like a beautiful decoration set in its parklike grounds. Even the barred windows of the sanctuary building had lost their ominous quality.

The Khan and C.V. Soong rose from their cushions in the Khan's lush Oriental office. With the drapes drawn open and the sunlight streaming in through open windows, all shadows were dispelled here too.

Old Soong greeted Chan with an outstretched hand.

"I was beginning to worry, Inspector," Soong beamed. "I should have known better. In the hands of Charlie Chan, all is safe."

"Some private business detained me," Chan said, "but I'm glad to say the scroll is now delivered without incident."

He handed the brass-bound chest to the Khan.

"Many thanks, Mr. Chan," the Khan said. "It will be locked up at once. Have you learned any more about the tragic death of poor Benny?"

"No, I have not."

Soong shook his head. "I'm afraid I acted somewhat irrationally, Inspector. I realize now that I'm not really sure those men were following me. The scroll made me jumpy, eh?"

"Valuable treasures are often difficult to live

with," Chan said. He turned to the Khan. "You are sure all the other scrolls sent previously are safe?"

"Oh, yes. Quite safe."

"Could some attempt have been made to steal them without you being aware of it? Some small incident overlooked, some insignificant evidence of unexpected visitors?"

"No," the Khan shook his head. "Not that I know. We are very concerned about our privacy here, Mr. Chan, and remain alert for anything unusual. Alas, it is necessary because the local residents do not always like us in their midst, and we must be vigilant for any intrusions."

Chan nodded. "But it is odd. The theft of a single apple from a prize tree is very rare. Thieves do not often take one jewel from a large box and leave all the others."

"I'm sure that no one tried to steal the scroll," the Khan said. "Poor Benny would not have resisted."

"You are sure Benny Chan would not resist a thief?" Chan asked.

"I'm fairly sure," the Khan said. "In many ways Benny was as intelligent as anyone—when the problem didn't confuse him. He read the newspapers, and he knew that it was best not to resist a theft or mugging. Then, too, Mr. Chan, he was timid, as most retarded are."

"What would make him resist, or perhaps confuse him and make him unsure whether to resist or run or both?"

"Any conflict of choice, Inspector. The same thing that confuses all of us, only with Benny it was more acute. Mostly, I'd think he could only attack if he felt it threatened someone else he valued or loved."

"You mean," Chan said, "Benny would have been most likely to resist danger if something he was loyal to was in danger also?"

"Yes, that's just what I mean. Like most of his kind, he was fiercely loyal. He would have been very confused by a conflict of fear for himself and fear for someone he loved."

"Such as his sister," Chan said, "or the Temple of the Golden Horde?"

The Khan nodded slowly, watching Chan. "Yes, Benny was very loyal to us, and to me personally. If we were threatened, I think he would have tried to fight, poor man. But I don't see in what way we could have been in danger."

"Perhaps it was the thought of losing the scroll?" C.V. Soong said.

The Khan shook his head. "No, Benny knew we valued the scrolls greatly, but I don't believe the loss of one scroll would have made him feel we were in danger."

"But what else could there have been?" Soong said.

The Khan shrugged. "I don't know. Nothing. No, I have to think that Benny died fleeing from his own private demons. What you in the West call an 'accident.' Tragic."

"Can private demons be seen by others?" Chan asked softly.

The Khan was silent. A furrow appeared between his dark eyes as if he were choosing the exact words he had to use to say what he had to say. At last he looked up at Chan,

"It would depend, Inspector, on what you think can be seen, and who was seeing. I believe the spirits are real, solid—they exist. You of the West do not believe the spirits are real—they are visions, hallucinations. For you to see them out in the night would not be possible. You would deny what you saw, refuse to see, call it illusion and unreality. For we who believe, we would see even if the demons came in a dream—it would be real."

"Is young Angela Smith one who would see?"

The Khan shook his head, "I do not know. She is a novice, still learning. The Snow Princess works with her, leads her belief, and I do not know how much she resists, how far she has come on the one true road."

"Perhaps now may be the time to find out," Chan said. "Can we visit her? Talk more?"

"Certainly," the Khan said. "Come along, Inspector Chan, Mr. Soong."

The three of them went out into the cool sun of the Northern California winter, and across the parklike grounds of the remote estate to the sanctuary building with its barred windows. In the hospital-like lobby, the burly female attendant in her dark kimono led them through the barred gate and along the silent corridors.

They turned a corner in the rear, and the attendant glanced back at them. "The Smith girl has not left her room this morningu. She is still under sedation after last night. But by now—"

She never finished. A tall man hurtled out of a doorway near the end of the corridor, and ran full tilt into her. Both went down in a flurry of arms, legs and flying kimono. The man was up first, already starting to run on. It was Carleton Sedgwick—wild-eyed and almost white.

"She's gone!" the lawyer cried, his voice almost in panic. "Gone! The door was open! We've got to—!"

The Khan restrained Sedgwick. "Stop! Calm yourself, Carleton! Tell us calmly." The Khan's eyes stared through him.

"Escaped!" Sedgwick said, and he took two deep breaths. "Angela, she's escaped from her room again! I must tell the Princess!"

"Of course, come," the Khan said. "We will find her. She cannot have gone far."

Sedgwick took another shuddering breath, forcing himself to calm down, but his eyes still jumped in a violent panic. Chan watched the lawyer. Why was the man so agitated? What was so dangerous to Sedgwick about the escape of a disturbed girl who had come to the Temple looking for peace?

The Khan, Soong, and Sedgwick hurried away along the corridor. Chan remained silently where he was. He saw that for the moment they had all forgotten him. When they were gone, he turned and went to the door from which Sedgwick had been running. It led to a small, narrow room furnished like a monk's cell. The single window was barred, with no space for a girl to squeeze through.

Chan looked at the door. There was a simple Yale lock, but it had been modified so that it could not be turned from inside. Chan looked at the mechanism, scowling. There was also a secondary bolt on the outside! Once locked, and bolted, there was no way out of the room.

Chan considered the door and the lock for some minutes, examined them closely, and found no marks of forcible exit.

Still scowling thoughtfully, the detective went inside and searched the almost bare room. On the single dresser sat a double frame with portrait photographs of a middle-aged man and woman, each photograph signed, "Love, Mother" and "Love, Dad."

There was nothing at all in three of the dresser drawers, and only a pitiful few underclothes and small accessories in the fourth drawer. And two envelopes addressed to Angela, both with a return address in Santa Barbara. The letters were missing from both envelopes.

Chan took one envelope and left the room. No one stopped him in the silent corridors. Outside, he walked in the sun toward his car. Far off near the pagoda he saw C.V. Soong alone. The Khan was nowhere in sight. But at the entrance to the office building, Carleton Sedgwick was waving his arms as he talked to the tiny Madame Li.

Chan watched them from the shade of a tall pine. The small woman seemed angry, speaking sharply to the lawyer. Suddenly she slapped the lawyer. He seemed to go rigid. They stood there for a moment, face to face like two animals at bay. Then Madame Li reached to touch Sedgwick's arm. She held to him a second, turned, and went into the building. Sedgwick followed her slowly.

Under the pine, Chan watched all this. He waited, but nothing more happened, and he went on to his car.

X

AT HIGHWAY PATROL Headquarters in Half Moon Bay, Lieutenant Forbes listened to Chan tell of Angela Smith.

"You should have reported that knife attack last night, Inspector," Forbes said.

"It was only the defensive action of a disturbed girl, not necessarily connected to the death of Benny Chan," Chan said. He smiled. "Also, you have given me permission to work on the case. A detective at work does not report all incidents at once."

"So I did." Forbes grinned. "Okay, Mr. Chan, but do you think the girl really *did* see something connected to Benny Chan's death?"

"I don't know, but she spoke of a violation of the sacred scroll, and as far as we know now, only Benny Chan had the scroll before you found it abandoned on the beach. Whatever she meant by violation, who else but Benny could have done it? Who else could the girl have seen pursued by demons?"

"If he was pursued by anyone that night, they damn well must have been demons," Forbes said. "We've been over that ground twice, and we found no marks or footprints. And I can't find anyone who saw any strangers in the area that night. Ghosts, maybe?"

"Or skilled men, well-trained in remaining unseen," Chan said. "Wearing light sneakers designed to leave little trace in grass or on rocky ground."

"You know something I don't?" Forbes said.

"Hints, no more. And it is too early for guesses," Chan said. "But I suggest an urgent search to locate Angela Smith."

"We'll get right on it," Forbes agreed. "What will you do?"

Chan took out the envelope he had found in Angela Smith's room at the Temple. "Smith is a common name. A young girl sent to the Temple because she is sick is most likely to have letters from her family. Yet the only letters found are from someone with a different name." He read the return address on the envelope, "J. Farley, 1499 Tunnel Road, Santa Barbara. I think I will talk again to Betty Chan, to see if the name of Farley means anything to her."

"Let me know what she says," Forbes said.

Chan nodded, and went back out to his car. The late afternoon sun was going down now to the west over the ocean, and the chill of evening was settling over San Francisco as he reached his hotel again. He called Betty Chan at once. No answer again. He called The Kung Fu Tze Book Store. The clerk who answered said Miss Chan was out on an errand. He left a message, went up to shower and change his clothes, and then went down to the coffee shop for a quick meal.

He was finishing his tea when the bellboy paged him for a telephone call. He hurried to the phone.

"Betty?" he said. "I must see you."

There was a silence. Then a soft, shaking voice said, "It isn't Betty. Who is Betty? Do I know Betty?"

It was a woman's voice, a girl.

"Who is this, please?" Chan said.

The voice giggled. It was a woman's voice, a girl.

"I know Benny," she said. "Poor Benny Chan, who drowned in a dark ocean. But Benny couldn't drown, oh no? Not Benny! The demons, they made Benny drown! Yes! I . . ."

"What do you know about Benny Chan?"

The voice seemed to moan, as if the person on the other end were thrashing against ropes.

"Inspector? Are you Inspector Chan?"

"Yes, I am Charlie Chan," he said, and "Angela? You are Angela Smith? Please, where are you?"

"Where am I?" The voice was silent, and Chan

could almost see the girl looking all around her to find out where she was. "I'm here! Don't you know that? I'm here, I know that, I'm not crazy! Oh, no, not crazy, not yet! I saw! You hear? I saw!"

"You saw what, Angela?" Chan said gently, soothing.

"Saw him, you hear? What did I see? I don't know! Demons! But what were they? What did they want? Poor Benny, he ran and they ran and—" She broke off.

"Angela?" Chan said. "Tell me where you are."
Silence.

Then, "I have to talk to you, tell you!" she said. "Come to the motel. Now. I'm in the motel! Hurry, please!"

"I will be there. What motel is it, I forget?" Chan said.

"Why, the Big Basin Motel, of course. In Pescadero. I'll be waiting. Pescadero," she giggled, "what a funny name."

Then she was gone.

Chan hurried back, paid his bill, and walked swiftly out to his rented car. He drove south once more.

Chan first noticed the car behind him after he passed through Half Moon Bay. The headlights came suddenly from some side road just south of Half Moon Bay and remained there, making no attempt to catch or pass him even though he drove more slowly than most American drivers. Other cars sped around Chan over and over, but this one particular car remained behind him.

Night now, the ocean mist rolling in over Highway One, and the lights behind were diffused and ghostly in the wet air. Chan watched them for some miles, Pescadero not far ahead by now. Had Angela Smith called anyone else? Someone at the Temple near Half Moon Bay, perhaps? Told them she had called Chan? So they had watched for his Toyota and now followed?

Or was the car following only him, to see where he was going? It was necessary to find out, and as he drove he looked for a side road. He saw one to the right just five miles north of Pescadero and turned in quickly. He bounced along the rutted dirt of the rural road toward the sound of the surf.

Headlights came through the thickening mist behind him!

Chan drove on, searching for some cover, some haven to hide and observe the following car. The dirt road wound on, climbing as it neared the rocky cliffs above the ocean. The headlights followed, neither closing in nor slipping back. The narrow road took a sharp left turn, dropped down into a deep hollow, and turned right again around a giant boulder, where Chan saw a dark house off to the left.

Without hesitation, when the lights behind

disappeared for the moment around the curves and boulder, Chan turned off the road, switched off his car's headlights, and pulled to a stop in back of the dark house. He slipped from the little Toyota swiftly, flicked the safety off his pistol, and circled the house to the front, where he crouched alertly and watched the dirt road.

The car came around the boulder. It was a big, black Cadillac, he saw now. Its headlights probed the fog like deadly antennae as it moved forward slowly. Chan saw three vague heads all peering ahead in search of something—of his car!

Then the big car stopped in front of the dark house. The motor went off. The men sat there, headlights on but not moving, as if the three men in the car were listening. They were trained men, Chan thought. They had lost him, but instead of rushing around blindly, they sat listening for the sound of his engine.

Chan continued to watch.

The doors of the car suddenly opened, and two men got out. They stood for a moment, talking softly to each other, and then the third man joined them. The third man nodded, drew a pistol, and leaned against the car. The other two turned and went off around the far side of the dark house behind which Chan waited.

As silently as a ghost, Chan rose and padded forward, circling around behind the big car, keeping well hidden in fog. He crept up on the Cadillac. In the distance, he heard a car door open and close—the door of his own car, he supposed, which the other two men had now found. Soon they would be back.

Chan did not hesitate. Leaping forward, he was on the man at the car like a great cat before the man knew anything. With two quick moves of Tai-Chi-Chuan, the man lay on the ground unconscious, his pistol falling uselessly to one side. Chan peered close at the man's face—it looked like the fellow who had followed him earlier.

He wasted no time searching the man. Professionals like that never carried identification, he knew. Instead, he reached in through the car's window, started the ignition, switched on the head-lights, put it into drive, and sent it slowly ahead down the dirt road toward the sound of the ocean. Then he jumped back into the shadows and began to circle again toward the dark house.

The other two men came running from behind the house. They shouted into the night and ran straight toward the moving car.

It was a mistake. In their surprise, they forgot what they were there to do and pursued their own vehicle instead. Chan reached the dark house safely, climbed into his car, and waited.

On the road, the big Cadillac struck the guard rail some some five hundred yards away, lurched, and came to rest with its nose in a deep hollow, the engine still running. Chan saw the two men reach it and peer inside.

This was the chance he had been waiting for. He started his small Toyota, turned and accellerated in a screech of tires, and drove back along the dirt road.

Somewhere behind him, voices shouted. Too late, he thought with satisfaction. They could not catch him now.

Soon he was back on the highway, and now there were no headlights trailing him. He drove on to Pescadero and the Big Basin Motel.

In the fog it was a large, well-lighted motel on the north edge of the town, set back from the high-way around a blue-lighted pool. The fog wreathed it, and no one was in the pool that steamed in the cool night. Music came from a large coffee shop, and there was a warm pleasant atmosphere to the mist-haloed lights.

In the office an efficient young man shook his head when Chan asked for Angela Smith.

"No one registered by that name, sorry."

"I'm sure she is here," Chan insisted. "It is a po-lice matter, I am Inspector Chan. Miss Smith is a tall girl, in her early twenties. Pretty, long blond hair, brown eyes. She is, perhaps, quite nervous."

"Oh, sure, Inspector. That's Unit Five, regis-tered as a Miss Jones. There isn't any trouble, is there? She seemed like a nice, quiet girl. She hasn't given us any trouble, and she had her dinner sent to her room."

"Where, please, is Unit Five?"

"Second from the end on the left, facing the pool."

Chan went out. A small car was parked in front of Unit Five—a car with the magical symbols of the Golden Horde drawn on its sides. Music came from inside Angela's room . . . and the voice of a man.

Chan knocked. The man's voice, he realized as he listened carefully to the words, had to be some actor on the television set. These new young people— even now the girl watched television!

When no answer came to his knock, Chan tried the door. It was unlocked, so he went in.

The TV set blared and flickered, the smiling actor talking to some woman not on the screen. Chan glanced all around. No one was in sight; the room was empty.

Water ran in the bathroom. His pistol out, Chan pushed open the bathroom door. No one was inside. He went out into the main room and looked into the two closets. They were empty. He saw the open rear window, went to it, and looked out.

Trees grew in a thick clump some ten yards behind the motel, and through the mist Chan saw something moving amongst them.

"Angela?" he called, waiting.

There was no answer, but the something moved

again—low under the trees, a figure that seemed to move and wait. Nervous, she must have gone to hide in the safety of the trees. Chan went out and around to the rear. He saw her.

She was standing erect under a tall redwood, barely moving, poised as if watching his every move.

Except that as he approached her he realized that she was too tall. Three feet too tall.

Too tall, and moving slowly from side to side, her head down, her arms loose and limp at her sides, swinging in the fog

Chan sighed as he looked up at her. The rope around her neck went over a branch of the redwood. A chair from the motel room lay on its side beneath her. She hung like a fruit on the tree. Dead.

Chan stood there for some moments before he picked up the chair, stood on it, and cut her down.

XI

THE POLICE PROBED through the brush under the trees, their floodlights turning the area behind the motel as bright as day in the ocean mist. The ambulance was there, the Coroner's man working over the body of Angela Smith, alias Jones, alias whatever her real name had been.

Forbes stood with Chan some distance away from where his men and the Sheriff's men were working. His tired eyes looked toward the dead girl, and then toward the dark trees, macabre now in the glare of the floodlights.

"Nothing in the bushes or in the room so far. Not a match that doesn't belong in the room—and nothing of the girl's. She must have come as she was. The car belongs to the Temple; they reported she'd taken it. If only we'd spotted it a few hours sooner." Forbes shook his head angrily, as if he had never gotten used to death even in his trade.

"The clerk at the desk saw no one, heard nothing?" Chan said.

"Not a thing." Forbes sighed. "It's a busy motel. It has a restaurant; people are coming and going all the time."

"An age of television. Who hears strange voices or noises over the actors blaring into the night?"

Forbes turned as the coroner's man came up. The medical examiner was drying his hands.

"Looks like strangulation, death by hanging. The chair's in the right place. About an hour ago, I'd say. Can I take her?"

"No other marks on her, Doctor?" Chan asked.

"You expect some?" the doctor said slowly.

"Possibly."

"Well, yes and no. She's got some bruises on her upper arms, small ones, could be old. A small swelling on her jaw. Nothing else. No rape or sex recently. Nothing under her fingernails."

Chan nodded, and Forbes motioned for the doctor to take Angela Smith's body. Then Forbes and Chan walked around the motel and into Unit Five. Forbes closed the door behind them, lit a cigarette, sat down, looked up at Chan.

"You don't believe it was suicide, Inspector Chan?" Forbes said. "A sick girl, almost crazy you said yourself. Highly on edge, neurotic, at the Temple to be calmed down. Rambling when she spoke to you on the telephone tonight. Probably paranoid, seeing demons. She tried to attack you with a knife. It looks like everything you'd expect of a suicidal kid."

"It would seem so, no evidence otherwise," Chan said, "except those bruises on her arms and the swelling on her jaw. No limbs of the tree were near enough to bruise her arms, and it is unlikely she fell and hit her own jaw."

"But she could have, and small bruises happen easily to a young girl."

"Tonight she insisted that I must meet her. She had something to tell me."

"Who knows what? Some crazy hallucination. Maybe she was so far out, she scared herself too much. It happens."

"Suicides happen, and accidents, but when both come together they cause great wonder. Also, it is strange when unknown men follow people involved with the accident and the suicide."

"All right, I agree. I wonder some, too," Forbes said. "I've got to admit that suicide fits everything I've heard about this Smith girl, but maybe it fits a little too well. Too easy an answer, like being handed it on a silver platter.

"And I wonder about a girl who runs away from a barred-window place, swipes a car, has no luggage—not even a handbag—and happens to bring a rope with her," Forbes said grimly. "There's no rope traces in the car, and the desk clerk says the girl never went out."

"Such facts give rise to questions," Chan agreed dryly.

"But if she was killed, why? By whom? What's the motive? What do we know, Mr. Chan?"

"I think the girl saw Benny Chan the night he died. I think she saw someone pursue the drowned handyman to the ocean."

"All right, then why was Benny drowned, if he was?"

"That, of course, is the question. If deaths are not what they seem, the cause is hidden well," Chan said. "Careful men in suits who have been following Betty Chan and C.V. Soong have made no moves, appear to be only watching. They may be agents of China or Russia, but if so, they have made no apparent attempt to steal the scrolls except the one Benny carried. Even then, the theft—if tried—was bungled, and professional agents should not make such a mistake."

"Then what the hell are they after?"

"Cannot say yet. Perhaps they watch for something we do not yet know," Chan said slowly, "something that has not happened yet, or someone who has not yet appeared. Betty Chan thinks she has been observed, perhaps followed, by men other than the men in suits. Strange watchers who wear capes and wide hats and keep their faces hidden."

"Capes and wide hats?" Forbes said. His eyes went distant for a moment, remembering something. "We had a report, maybe a year ago, from the S.F.P.D. It was a general report, just for our information. Seems that the old Tongs are being revived up in San Francisco. Only a rumor, really, but we know the Tongs have made a comeback in Hong Kong, Singapore, Macao, and other places outside Red China where there are large Chinese population. Even in Taiwan, I've heard, despite Chiang's puritanism."

"Or because of it," Chan said. "I am aware of the unhappy revival of the Tong in those places. Terrorists and extortionists, criminals who live off their own people like the Mafia. I was not aware they had already reached San Francisco."

"Some of the S.F.P.D. say they have, only a few gangs right now, but maybe growing," Forbes said, and he looked at Chan. "I hear that one of the Tongs calls itself the Yellow Claw Society after one of the old Tongs, and they wear capes and wide hats!"

Chan was silent for a long minute. His dark eyes seemed to be seeing the pain and sorrow of the past caused by the old Tong Societies and their blood feuds and terrorism. It was one of the sadder moments in the history of his people—lost strangers in a strange land where they weren't welcome, hounded by everyone, and then robbed and murdered by their own gangsters.

"Why would a Tong be connected with Benny Chan?" he asked.

"The scroll?" Forbes wondered.

"It would not seem likely, and gangsters would not have lost the box on an open beach," Chan said. "No, Lieutenant, there is much here as yet unexplained."

"Could Benny have been a member of a Tong? Or the sister? Maybe your impossible Chinese agents are interested in the Tong for some reason, and know a connection between Benny and the Tong."

Chan nodded sadly. "It is always possible. Fear of Tong vengeance might have been greater than the fear of water in Benny Chan. I think it is time to change actions to bring hidden forces into the open."

"How, Mr. Chan?"

"I think there is a way," Chan said, his voice grim now. "C.V. Soong has given me a thought. Benny Chan was carrying the fifth scroll when he drowned. The sixth scroll is still in Honolulu. Perhaps the man who brings the sixth scroll from Hawaii to the Temple will also be a target. A target more alert than Benny Chan."

"You mean yourself?" Forbes asked. "I don't know; it's risky."

"Tiger trap must be baited with lamb. Only this lamb can be a disguised wolf. A slight disguise, known to none, will hide detective. We will tell only that the scroll is coming to San Francisco by some messenger. See what tigers rise to bait."

"Will Soong go for that? He values those scrolls a lot."

"We will tell Soong only that I will deliver the next scroll, not our other plans."

"I don't know, Inspector. We don't know what we're dealing with here," Forbes said.

"Perhaps nothing at all," Chan said. "But we must find out. To catch an unseen shark, it is necessary to bait our hook with the best morsel."

"Be careful, Mr. Chan," Forbes said. "Just be very careful."

XII

C.V. SOONG was delighted by Charlie Chan's offer to bring the last scroll from Hawaii to the Temple of the Golden Horde, and, when Chan had finished his last day at the International Penology Symposium, the detective flew back to Honolulu.

After a day with his family in the house on Punchbowl Hill, Chan drove his sedate old 1949 Cadillac to the philanthropist's house. A slim Chinese maid wearing traditional Chinese dress ushered him into the rich library of the vast mansion. A stocky man with a thin smile greeted Chan.

"Inspector Chan? I'm George Hastings, Mr. Soong's executive assistant."

The stocky man shook hands. He had a soft, fat hand that matched his full face and fleshy mouth. But Hastings's eyes were small and sharp.

Chan inclined his head in a small bow.

"Honored," he murmured.

"I'm the one who's honored," Hastings said, smiling. "I've long wanted to meet you, Inspector. Mr. Soong is most grateful for your offer of help, and so am I."

"Ah? Why are *you* grateful, Mr. Hastings?"

"I'm pleased by anything that helps Mr. Soong," the assistant said somewhat stiffly.

"Most commendable," Chan said dryly. "Were you acquainted with the former messenger, Benny Chan?"

"Yes, I was. As a matter of fact, I gave him the box with the scroll each time. There was no trouble until the last trip. I really can't imagine how he could have been so careless as to almost lose the scroll!"

"Was anything different about the fifth scroll, or about the trip Benny Chan made to the mainland?"

"Nothing at all. I never deviate from normal routine, Mr. Chan," Hastings said, not as pleased by Chan anymore, it seemed.

"Who would have taken the sixth scroll if I had not?"

Hastings seemed to grow rigid, his small eyes like dark points. "Why, I think perhaps I would have—"

Before Chan could continue with George Hastings, the library door opened and C.V. Soong came in. He wore his Oriental robes again, and he wasn't alone. Madame Li stood behind him, small and wearing western dress now. In the slim, short skirt she seemed younger, her figure lithe and shapely.

"Ah, Inspector, this is very kind of you," C.V. Soong said, beaming as he walked up to Chan. "I feel completely relieved. The shipping of the sixth scroll has been preying on my mind."

"Mr. Hastings would probably have been a reliable courier," Chan said.

"Yes, George is reliable, but I'm not sure how he would handle a physical attack," Soong said. "Madame Li came to take the sixth scroll herself, unaware that you had offered. I'm sure that she, too, is relieved."

"Inspector Chan is generous to help us," the tiny woman said. "In his hands, what could happen to the scroll?"

Chan smiled to the cult Princess, but behind his quiet eyes his mind wondered if there wasn't, perhaps, a veiled threat in her words. He noted that C.V. Soong did not seem to hear anything unusual.

"Exactly!" the old philanthropist beamed.

"Perhaps we should get the scroll now, Mr. Soong. I have other business," Madame Li said. "I would like to be sure it is in the box when Inspector Chan leaves."

"Of course, my dear," Mr. Soong agreed.

"George, will you get the box, please?"

While his stocky assistant was out of the room, C.V. Soong chatted about the long history of the scrolls and how they had been in his family for three generations. Chan listened politely, but he was watching Madame Li. Did the tiny woman suspect C.V. Soong of something? Had she some reason to think that the scroll might not be in the box? Or could it be that there was something wrong about the scrolls? Fakes? Chan had not considered that possibility.

If there was anything wrong with his scrolls, C.V. Soong seemed to be unworried. He went on talking about the six priceless historical documents until Hastings returned with a heavy dark wood chest exactly like the one Benny Chan had carried. Its brass fittings gleamed.

"Open it, Hastings," Soong said. There was an almost hushed reverence in his voice. If the scroll was a fake, Soong was putting on a good act.

"Please," Chan said quickly, "allow me to open it. I ought to be familiar with the box, its contents, and the lock."

Hastings handed him the key. It was large, made of brass, very ancient, and fitted the massive old lock loosely. But for all its formidable appearance, Chan saw it could be simply and easily opened with almost any flat, cabinet-type key—or not much more than a well-handled hairpin.

He opened the chest.

The scroll lay inside on its two polished spindles exactly like the fifth scroll. Soong removed it reverently and unrolled a section. He and Madame Li examined it. The tiny woman nodded, and Soong returned it to the chest. Chan locked it, pocketing the key.

"I will now assume full responsibility for scroll and its safe delivery to Temple. May I suggest the Khan be there to meet me? I will go to San Francisco by my own route, take all my own precautions. That way no one knows where, how, or when the scroll will arrive. I suggest Madame Li and Mr. Soong go to San Francisco also; perhaps potential thieves will follow them."

"Excellent, Inspector," Soong agreed.

With a small nod to each of them, Chan left the library. He stood for a moment in the vast entry hall, listening. He heard nothing, though, and went on out of the big house. As he climbed into his immaculate old Cadillac, placing the chest on the seat beside him, he saw a figure at the corner of the grandiose old mansion.

Someone was watching from among the tall palms and the thick hibiscus!

Chan started his car and drove on down the curving shell drive of the Hawaiian estate. He didn't even glance toward the palms and thick flowers at the corner of the house as he passed. But the moment he was out of sight, he stopped the car, drew his small pistol, got out, and slipped back through the palms and banana trees. The figure was still at the corner of the house.

Chan unwittingly stepped on a liana, caught his foot, and the noise of the vine rustling heavily echoed through the day. The man at the corner of the house whirled—it was Carleton Sedgwick. Before Chan could move or call out, the tall lawyer ran around the house and vanished.

Chan began to run in pursuit—and stopped. The scroll was back in his car! Could Sedgwick be a ruse to lure him away from his charge before he had even started his trip?

Quickly, the detective hurried back through the trees and thick bushes to his Cadillac.

The box was still there. He opened it with the key. As far as he could tell, the scroll was undisturbed. Thoughtfully, Chan climbed once more into his ear and drove slowly off. What had Carleton Sedgwick been doing lurking near Soong's mansion?

Nothing more happened, and Chan drove home to leave his car and tell Madame Chan that once more he was leaving for a time.

Later that day, he took a taxi to his downtown office, observing no one suspicious among the throngs of mixed ancestry of the island state. In his office he made reservations on jets at three different airlines, at three different times. Carrying the box, he left his office in an official car in time to make the first flight he had reserved on. He dismissed the police car and walked into the main terminal building.

Inside, he checked in at the flight desk, confirmed his reservation, then went into the men's room, still carrying the brass-bound chest. Once in the men's room he waited until he was alone, then quickly used a key on a side door that led from the lavatory into a narrow rear hall. It was a trick he had used before.

Unobserved in the deserted rear hall, Chan left the terminal carefully and entered a nearby hangar. There he went into a small room and opened a black case he had put there some hours before he went to C.V. Soong's house. He went to work.

Twenty minutes later a portly Chinese with a small beard and dark glasses came out of the room wearing a black Mao suit. The apparent Chinese businessman or official carried a brown canvas suitcase of the type favored by proletarian functionaries, and a chest under his arm. He went back to the front of the terminal building and caught a taxi into Honolulu.

Once downtown again, Chan, in his disguise, had lunch at a small restaurant he knew well. He appeared oblivious to all that went on in the restaurant, but actually observed everyone who entered or left. He saw no one suspicious. His meal finished, he left and caught another taxi back to the airport in time to catch the second of the three flights on which he had reserved passage.

On the jet, he sat quietly in his seat, assuming an air of aloof disdain for his fellow travelers as he buries himself in a book. It was a common sight, and few people did more than glance at him once.

He remained quiet and wary the entire flight, but no one came near him, and he saw no one watching him. He recognized none of the passengers, not the cautious men in the dark suits, nor anyone who looked like the member of a Tong gang. By the time the jet landed in San Francisco, Chan was sure that no one could have followed him or been waiting for him.

From the San Francisco airport, he took a taxi to a second-class hotel downtown near the bay, The Moreton. It was a hotel where Inspector Charlie Chan had never stayed, where no one who knew him would ever look for him. He checked in, then went up to his room. He was now in San Francisco, and no one knew he was here. No one knew where the box was with the scroll in it.

Anyone who wanted to steal the scroll would have to be waiting somewhere near the Temple of the Golden Horde for him to appear carrying the brass-bound chest. When, and if, they did, Chan and the local police would be ready. The trap was set and baited.

For tomorrow.

Tonight Chan had nothing to do but relax while everyone else sweated and wondered where he was.

He showered, then went down to an obscure restaurant he knew where they had excellent Chinese cuisine. Feeling pleased with his efforts, he treated himself to the best Mandarin duck, delicately fried shrimp with none of the Cantonese thick crust of batter, and crisp Mandarin vegetables.

After dinner he went for a stroll in the foggy winter night near the bay. All that remained to do was contact Lieutenant Forbes and complete the trap. When he returned to his room he felt sure that tomorrow he would know, one way or the other, if Benny Chan and Angela Smith had died for the sacred scrolls.

Humming to himself, he stepped into his room—and saw too late that his canvas suitcase was open!

Then an arm went around his throat, thin and muscular, and the hand pressed his neck in a skilled judo attack.

XIII

CHARLIE CHAN lay in near darkness, unmoving. He was on the floor of his hotel room, he realized, and he held himself carefully immobile while his keen senses probed out to assess his situation. There was no sound, no movement in the room, and yet he sensed he was not alone. Someone was with him.

Very slowly, Chan let his eyes look all around. Finally, his glance rested on a chair far across the darkened room. The faint glow of streetlight penetrated at the edges of the curtained windows, revealing a shape seated there.

Chan waited. He didn't move a muscle. The figure in the chair didn't move, either. Chan tried to quiet his breathing and listen. He heard nothing. Still the figure across the dark room never moved.

Quickly, Chan stood up and flicked the light switch in one fluid movement.

The Khan, Li Po, sat in an armchair across the room. The thin leader of the Golden Horde seemed to be scowling at Chan. But he wasn't. He wasn't scowling at anything. The golden hilt of a Chinese dagger protruded from his chest.

Chan crossed quickly to him. There was no need for haste, he saw. Blood covered the front of Li Po's Oriental robe. The Khan was dead.

For a moment, Chan stood there unbelieving. How had the killer found him? How had the Khan found him? Why? He reached out to touch the dead man. The Khan's body was still warm. No more than twenty minutes, perhaps less.

Chan whirled. The chest was gone! The killer had taken the scroll, but what had the Khan been doing in the hotel room in the first place? Following someone he had discovered was trying to steal the sacred scrolls, caught that person in the act, and so been killed?

But how had the thief, the killer, anyone, located the scroll? How had anyone found him? Chan remained certain he could not have been followed—and yet, he must have been.

Grimly, Chan turned to the telephone, picked up the receiver, and called the police. He asked for Captain Wade, then gave his name. Wade came on at once.

"Charlie? This is the social call? Where do we meet?"

"Sorry to say, this isn't social, Mort. Very much business. I'm in a room at The Moreton Hotel. I've got a dead body with me; the Khan of that Golden Horde Temple. You had better come with your people."

"In your room?"

"Yes, my room. Also, there has been a theft—"

Chan stopped, blinked. He stared across the room to a dark corner behind the bed.

"Charlie?" Captain Mort Wade said from the other end of the line. "Are you okay? Charlie?"

"Yes, I am fine. Come quickly!"

"On my way."

Chan hung up, then crossed to the corner. He stared down. The brass-bound chest sat on the floor.

Chan blinked slowly, like an owl. Then he bent and saw that the key rested in the lock. He opened the lid. The scroll lay inside, intact.

He stood up slowly, looked at the box, then at the dead Khan, and a puzzled expression settled on his pale ivory face. He remained in deep thought until the police arrived.

Captain Mort Wade watched the Medical Examiner's men take out the body of Li Po, Khan of the Temple of the Golden Horde.

"Single knife wound in the heart," Wade told Chan. "It never made a sound when it hit, the M.E. says. Obviously the work of someone who knew how to use a knife. About an hour ago now. Does that put the time about when you were attacked?"

"Very close, yes," Chan said. "The man who attacked me also knew how to use judo and karate. He pressured the exactly proper point on my neck to render me unconscious."

"So far no reports from the hotel on seeing anyone," Wade said. "From the sound of the killer or killers, I've got a hunch we won't be getting any reports. An expert job. A professional."

"Someone trained in the martial arts," Chan said quietly. "Like an agent of intelligence-service, or a Tong assassin."

"Yeah," Wade agreed.

Suddenly weary, Chan seated himself at the room's small table. The place that was full of San Francisco policemen now. Wade sat facing him. The Captain seemed worried, puzzled.

"You came here from Honolulu carrying the scroll, sure no one followed you. Yet you were attacked in this room, and the Khan was murdered here."

"I used every skill to be sure no one followed, but obviously my skills were not good enough," Chan said.

"No, I don't believe that Charlie. If you made sure no one could follow you, then no one could have. You're too good to make some stupid mistake. Your idea was to set yourself up as bait to see if anyone would try to steal the scroll?"

"The plan was to begin tomorrow," Chan said. "The shark struck before the bait was out, and it is now clear that the theft of these scrolls is not the aim of killer."

"I guess not," Wade agreed. "Then what is behind it all? Something to do with that Temple? Some enemy of the cult? Maybe something they were doing down there?"

"All three victims were closely associated with the Temple of the Golden Horde," Chan observed. "Each murder points more to some motive close to cult. Have you any results of the investigations I requested, Captain?"

"As a matter of fact, I do," Wade said. "I was getting a report typed up tomorrow to send to you in Honolulu, but I can give you most of it right now."

"Please do so!"

The Captain opened his notebook. "Nothing much on Betty Chan. Born here, went to high school in Chinatown, was married briefly to a kid name Jang Shi, but it didn't take, she got it annulled after a few months. The kid's real name was George Shi, he Chinese-ized it when he ran with a street gang in Chinatown. Anyway, the Chan girl broke up the marriage, got a couple of waitress jobs, and finally ended up in that bookstore. It's kind of a Chinese Culture bookstore, they seem to like her there, and that's it. No record, no past troubles I know of."

"Where is her ex-husband?"

"No idea, he seems to have faded out. It wasn't much of a marriage; the boy doesn't seem to have ever held a job. If he's still around Chinatown, he's in the shadows. That's not so hard to do down there."

"It can be a labyrinth," Chan said thoughtfully. "What, then, of Madame Li and Carleton Sedgwick?"

"Not much on Madame Li. She only married the Khan a few years ago, came up from Los Angeles, and we're still checking," Wade said, "but Sedgwick's something else. He came from back East maybe ten years ago after a shady deal involving stock manipulations. Not enough to get him disbarred, or jailed, but the kind of deal that got him fired by a blue-ribbon law firm. Seems he was a real law-school hotshot, was taken on by this topflight firm. After about two years they caught him pulling a deal for himself on hush-hush info he got in a client relationship."

"Do you have details?"

"What he actually did was conduct negotiations to buy a block of apartments for a client, only under the table he helped fix it so some outside friends of his got the property! He took his cut, of course, and he also got canned for unethical conduct."

"Most interesting," Chan murmured.

"He showed up in Los Angeles, opened his own firm, and moved into Beverly Hills. For a year or so he seemed okay, then he started handling, ah, some disreputable clients. Shady car dealers, some of the barred-room boys with 'sanitariums' that are nothing but drunk cures, a few hoods, two stock shysters who were caught in illegal deals and went to jail."

"Was Sedgwick ever indicted?" Chan asked.

"No. He's smart and slick and has very sticky fingers. He's still got his office down in L.A., and they consider him a bit of a con-man there, but nobody has ever made any charges stick. About two years ago he showed up here, opened a sub-office, and took on representing the Temple down at Half Moon Bay. We've never had a complaint here, but he's a boy who likes a fast buck."

"Very helpful," Chan said. "To me it seemed that he is very close to Madame Li. With the Khan dead, I wonder who will take over the cult?"

"I guess we'll have to find out. Is there any money to be made running it, I wonder?" Wade said.

"It is a thought," Chan agreed. "Was there any indication that Madame Li and Sedgwick might have known each other previously? Both, I note, were in Los Angeles not too many years ago."

"Well, none that we found so far, but Sedgwick did show up around the Temple soon after Madame Li married the Khan. What made her eligible to be the 'Snow Princess' of the cult anyway? Does that go with the marriage?"

"I do not know," Chan said. "Possibly an inquiry

to L.A. might be in order. I would like to learn if the Temple of the Golden Horde has any associations down there."

"Will do," Wade said. He made a note in his notebook.

Chan rubbed at his nose for a moment. "You mentioned Mr. Sedgwick being involved in a sanitarium, one of the barred-room operations?"

"He was. Unlicensed home for sick rich people, mostly a high-priced drunk cure. A hide-out for 'sick' crooks, a place to keep rich Uncle Joe out of the way while you use his money. That kind of operation."

Chan nodded. "I wonder—"

"Captain!"

Wade and Chan turned quickly. One of Wade's detectives stood in the room doorway. He carried the brass-bound chest of the scroll. He came toward the Captain.

"Cap'n, did I hear Inspector Chan say he doesn't know how anyone found him in this hotel?"

"Yeah," Wade said. "If I know Charlie, no one—"

Chan said, "Perhaps the detective knows how I was found?"

"Yeah," the detective said, "I think I do."

The detective placed the brass-bound chest on a table, then touched one of the brass plates on the corner. "Here," he said. "Take a close look at it."

Chan bent close to the brad indicated. Brass-capped like the others, it seemed no different, except that it appeared to be loose. Carefully, Chan inserted a fingernail under the hood and, wiggling it, managed to pull the brad out. The stem formed a miniature signal device.

"At the airport," the detective said, "they only had to follow the signal."

Chad nodded, went on staring at the small chest. "Child's play to wait at the airport for all Honolulu flights and hear the signal no matter what disguise I wore."

Wade took the device, looked at it, then at the chest. "So someone in Honolulu marked the chest. Who, Charlie?"

"Any of those present in house of C.V. Soong—Madame Li, assistant George Hastings, Mr. Soong himself, or Carleton Sedgwick who was on the grounds."

"But Betty Chan must be clear, then, right?" Wade said.

"Not necessarily," Chan said. "Hastings could be an accomplice, also after the chest. He might have relayed the information to Betty Chan in San Francisco."

"And Madame Li could have fixed it for the Khan," Wade said. "He came to get it, undercover. The one person no one would suspect because it was going to him anyway. Only something went bad."

"Possibly," Chan nodded.

The detective who had found the device said,

"We just got more word on that Madame Li, Captain. Seems she was leader of her own cult down in L.A. a few years ago—The China Rebirth Society. It was getting a hold in the Chinese community, taking in some Vietnamese and a few Japanese, when they got busted for illegal drug use in their ceremonies. Seems they were building the faith by zonking out some of their richer devotees."

"Drugs?" Wade snapped. "What kind and where were they getting the stuff?"

"Mostly opium; they smoked up a storm in their ceremonies. Don't know the source, never traced it."

Charlie Chan was staring again at the heavy, brass-bound chest that carried the priceless scroll. His hooded eyes blinked very slowly. Captain Wade saw him, and turned to look at the box himself. Chan reached out and took the box, he began to turn it slowly in his hands.

"Six scrolls come to San Francisco in six boxes. Priceless scrolls no one can sell easily; therefore it's unlikely anyone would want to steal them. Very important contents, and everyone examines them, but who looks at the chests?"

He went on turning the heavy little chest in his delicate hands, his fingers feeling and probing like a surgeon, his dark eyes narrowed to observe every chink and blemish and fitting on the box. His fingers moved, pressed, felt, until there came a faint sound of metal moving. Only a hair, but one brass plate on a corner moved with a tiny click.

Wade stared. "You think—?"

Chan said nothing. He bent close to where the small plate had moved. He pushed, and the whole end of the box slid a quarter of an inch. Pushed again in all directions, delicately, and the end of the box slid up a full inch! Once more, sliding the panel sideways, he slid it off completely, revealing a hidden space no more than a half an inch deep but across the entire end of the box.

"Ancient Chinese were very clever at making secret boxes. Common child's toy, but many boxes were made that were not child's toys. Very cunning work, and it leaves nothing revealed to even the sharpest eye."

Captain Wade took the box and looked at the revealed opening. He rubbed a finger in one corner of the narrow cavity. He put that finger to his lips, licked it lightly. He nodded to Chan.

"Heroin, Charlie. I'm sure, but I'll have it analyzed at the lab anyway. There was heroin in this box."

Chan thought for a moment. "Benny Chan carried five boxes into this country. Four arrived without incident at the Temple of the Golden Horde. The fifth caused the death of Benny Chan and was dropped on the beach. Why?"

"You know?"

"Perhaps," Chan said. "Angela Smith was violent and hysterical about the 'demons' that pursued Benny Chan. She raved about a 'violation' of sacred scroll, about 'him' violating the scroll. I think she saw Benny Chan open the box. He may have opened the secret panel by mistake and seen the contents. Confused, not knowing whether to report it, afraid of danger to his loved Temple . . ."

"And whoever was to get the heroin spotted Benny, chased him, and drowned him!" Wade exclaimed.

"That would seem the answer."

"Who, Charlie?"

"I think only Miss Angela Smith can tell us."

"How?"

"At the moment, this is only a guess in the dark. Possibly the box will tell us more, including the source of the heroin. You will investigate both areas, Mort?"

"Okay, and you?"

"I think I will take a small trip. I will return by tomorrow."

XIV

FROM THE AIRPORT in Santa Barbara, Charlie Chan took a taxi to a motel on upper State Street, and went to bed. He left a wake-up call for seven A.M. He wanted to be at work early in the morning.

The next day, after a quick breakfast, he rented a car and drove out past the old mission to Foothill Road. He drove toward the Botanic Gardens until he reached Tunnel Road. Number 1499 was a large old Spanish-style mansion of adobe brick and red-tiled roofs. Its rich grounds stretched lushly up the steep slope of the mountains, and in the clear winter morning, he saw two gardeners working in the distance.

Two cars were in the garage. Mr. and Mrs. J. Farley seemed to be home, which was why Chan had come so early—to be sure. He parked and walked up to the heavy front door. He had to ring three times before he finally heard movement inside, a slow, light movement approaching the door.

The woman who opened the door was tall, blond, and in her late forties, but looked older, drawn, the deep furrows of some suffering on her handsome face. Her eyes had some of the manic look of Angela Smith, half crazy, and physically she resembled the dead girl, too.

"Yes?" she said, her voice low and dull.

"Mrs. Farley?" Chan said. "My name is Charlie Chan. I am working on the murder of your daughter. May I come in?"

"Chan?" the woman said, blinked. "Murder?" She blinked again, her manic eyes looking around him and past him as if for something she could understand. "They were Chinese. That Snow Princess, she's Chinese. What are you doing here?" She shook her head as if to clear a fog. "No, suicide they said."

"I'm sorry, the police now think it was murder. Your daughter was disturbed. She went to seek peace at the Temple of the Golden Horde. Did you speak with her in the last days?"

A man appeared in the long, cool, stone-floored entry hall behind the woman. A big, heavy man with almost white hair and wearing rough western clothes.

"Went?" the man said. "No, Angela didn't go to that Temple—we sent her! God damn us, we sent her!"

"James," the woman said, turned. "Please. How could we know? We did what we thought best."

The man, James Farley, laughed. "I wonder how many crimes have been done under that slogan; we did what we thought best! Best for whom? Eh? Whose best were we thinking of!"

"We were thinking of Angela!" the woman cried.

"Sure," the man said bitterly. He looked at Chan. "You want to know about Angela's death? About that Madame Li? About us, the smart parents? You're a cop?"

"Inspector Chan, yes," Chan said. "You are Mr. Farley, the father of the dead girl?"

"Stepfather, God help me," the man said, his voice cracking. He stared at Chan, then nodded, "Come on in. I'll tell you about Angela."

Farley led Chan and the woman into a vast, low living room with dark ceiling beams and rich old Spanish furniture. They were horse people, Chan could see, and the detective also saw that there was a lot of money. Farley waved him to a high-backed Spanish arm chair. The woman sat on the very edge of another chair. Farley remained standing, and he began to pace.

"Angela was my wife's child by her first marriage. I adopted her legally, but she never really liked me, you see?" Farley said. "Why should she? Who says a child has to like the man her mother marries after dumping her father?"

"James, please," Mrs. Farley said. "Don't whip yourself—"

Farley didn't seem to hear her; he went on pacing.

"She was unhappy, wild, always in trouble," he continued. "Oh, nothing terrible; just hard to handle, you know? An annoyance!" He went on pacing. "Then a few months ago she ran off with a young punk, stole a car, was picked up drunk. We paid the boy off, but she was pregnant. We got her an abortion and sent her off to Madame Li. For her own good, right?"

"She was disturbed, James! Sick. She needed help!" Mrs. Farley cried.

"Disturbed, sure, but not sick. She needed help, all right, but not the kind we gave her!" Farley said "I'd heard about Madame Li and her 'Sanctuary Retreat' at that Golden Horde Temple from a friend in Los Angeles who'd had trouble with one of his boys. He told us Madame Li specialized in helping disturbed kids by spiritual treatment at her Temple, especially kids who wouldn't listen to their parents. For a price, of course. A big price, but she guaranteed they would find peace and give no more trouble or worry. So we sent Angela to find peace, and she found it, didn't she?"

"James, no, please," Mrs. Farley moaned, wringing her hands. "We couldn't know what was going to happen."

"No, we couldn't know that, but we knew what we were doing! We were sweeping her under the rug, getting her off our backs! So we could have peace! For us! Madame Li's sanctuary is a private prison, isn't it! A very expensive private prison for rich parents who want their defiant children restrained! The spiritual treatment is drugs, brainwashing, and barred windows! The peace of fear and locked doors, all guaranteed! No more trouble or worry for the parents! A racket to handle kids the easy way, keep them locked up and out of trouble!"

Chan said softly, "You can prove this? Madame Li uses drugs, physical restraint?"

"Of course we can prove it!" Farley snapped. Then he stopped pacing, looked at Chan. "You said . . . murder. Are you sure? You know why? Or who?"

"Did Angela talk to you before she escaped from the Temple? A phone call? Letter? Any word?" Chan asked.

"No, nothing," Farley said.

"We . . . we weren't supposed to contact Angela too often," Mrs. Farley said. "That was part of the treatment."

"Why did she use a false name? Was that part of the treatment, too?" the detective asked.

"Yes," Farley said. "They called it assuming a new identity in the spirit realm, but I knew all along it was just a safety measure for them in case anyone came snooping around. My God, what did we put that girl through!" The man sat down now, holding his head in his hands.

"Sometimes mistakes are made," Chan said gently. "The question now is why was Angela murdered? I think she saw something. Do either of you know what it could have been?"

Mrs. Farley shook her head. "We hadn't spoken to Angela in nearly a month. They sent us reports, but we were supposed to keep away."

"They?" Chan said.

"That Sedgwick does most of the talking, the business," Farley said. "You're sure Angela was murdered, Inspector Chan? I mean . . . why?"

"Fairly certain. Motive? Perhaps to keep her quiet," Chan replied.

"Yes," Farley said. His haggard face seemed, for an instant, almost happier. "At least, maybe she didn't kill herself. Maybe we didn't drive her to that. It's something to know."

"Possibly Angela was coming to you when she was murdered," Chan said. "She may have been drugged, but not broken. She wanted to tell me something. She wanted to help the police; she was a strong girl."

The two Farleys looked like people Chan had just given a million dollars tax-free. Hope in their faces that perhaps their daughter had not been broken, suffering and suicidal.

"I wish we could help more," Farley said.

"Perhaps you have helped enough," Chan said. "There is now a motive for murder."

XV

WHEN HE ARRIVED back at the San Francisco airport, Charlie Chan noticed the two silent men in dark business suits who followed him casually out of the terminal. He gave no indication he had seen them, but went straight to police headquarters downtown. In Captain Wade's office he made three telephone calls: to Lieutenant Forbes in Half Moon Bay, to the Temple to say he was bringing down the scroll, and to Betty Chan.

"The solution is close," he told the girl. "I'll pick you up at the bookstore in half an hour."

"Where are we going, Inspector Chan?" the girl asked, her voice a shade wary.

"To offer condolences at the Temple of the Golden Horde—and reveal a murderer."

"I'll be ready," Betty Chan said determinedly.

*   *   *

An hour later, as the evening shadows began to fall, Captain Wade turned the police car into the side road that led to the isolated Templeh. The night fog drifted in from the ocean through the silent trees. The high iron gates were locked, so Wade parked outside. They used the small side gate and walked again up the curving gravel drive toward the three main buildings.

A figure came out of the fog and shadows from the direction of the main headquarters of the cult. It was C.V. Soong. The old philanthropist seemed pale and drawn as he hurried up to Chan, Captain Wade, and Betty Chan.

"Inspector Chan! What happened? Madame Li called me in Honolulu to tell me the terrible news about the Khan, and that the scroll hadn't been delivered!"

Chan's voice was mild, "The scroll is safe in the hands of the original messenger." He held out the brass-bound chest.

Soong sighed in relief as he reached for the small chest.

"Thank God! I'm sorry, Inspector, I shouldn't have doubted that you'd get it through safely, no matter what happened."

"Your praise is not deserved," Chan said. "The killer caught me by surprise and could easily have stolen the box."

"Well, no matter," Soong said, "I've got the

scroll, and all six are safe!" The old scholar-tycoon frowned. "But if it wasn't the scroll, why was the Khan murdered? Does this mean that Benny Chan and the Smith girl were also murdered?"

Betty Chan said, "I knew my brother had been murdered all along! I told you all! And no one would listen."

"It would appear now that you were indeed correct," Chan said. "It remains only to find the killer and reveal the motive. Mr. Soong, where is Madame Li . . . and where is Carleton Sedgwick?"

"Madame Li is in the pagoda with the Khan's body," Soong said. "I haven't seen Sedgwick."

"Then I suggest we pay our last respects to the Khan," Chan said.

They all went into the pagoda through the round portal. Inside, the smell of incense was thick, and blue light flickered around the stone altar from small candles inside blue glasses. Among the symbols of forest and sky and the magical runes of the Mongol Shamans, the bier lay in front of the altar. In a heavy silence, Madame Li lay face down in front of it, dressed all in flowing white robes.

"Madame Li?" Chan said quietly.

The tiny woman didn't move. They waited. Her voice seemed to drift out of the gloom of the temple itself:

"You violate the spirits of the Temple. Have you no respect for the dead? Leave me to mourn the loss of our Khan and the death of my husband."

"To mourn is good," Chan said, "but to know is better. The parents of Angela Farley mourn also. Parents who paid much money to place their daughter in your care. A poor child who died because she saw what she was not supposed to see."

The woman still didn't move. "A child too disturbed, too sick to know what she saw."

"Disturbed, perhaps, a little," Chan said. "But more disturbed by being placed in your private prison, behind barred windows. Restrained against her will because her parents paid much for you to do so. Not sick, Madame Li, but drugged by you! Kept always drugged. Somehow she resisted, fooled you, and managed to escape."

Captain Wade said, "There are laws against that kind of operation."

For another moment the tiny woman lay there unmoving. Then she slowly got up and turned away from the bier of her dead husband to face Chan and Wade, C.V. Soong and Betty Chan.

"So you know?" she said. "All right, yes, we provided a service for people who wanted their hard-to-handle children cared for. But that's all!"

Chan said, "We know about the heroin shipped to the Temple hidden inside the chests. The heroin you used in your treatment of the disturbed children."

Madame Li blinked. "The chests?"

"The secret Benny Chan discovered accidentally and had to be killed to hide. Angela Farley saw Benny open the secret compartment—violate the scroll—and saw your killers pursue him. The Khan must have known what Angela saw, or perhaps he discovered the secret of the boxes himself."

"The Khan?" the tiny woman blinked again. "He . . . he did talk much to Angela, and he was checking the chests yesterday. I saw him! Was that why he was killed?"

"Who knows better than you!" Betty Chan cried. "Murderer! You killed my brother!"

"I killed no one!" Madame Li shook her head violently. "Yes, I used the Temple to make money from the stupid rich who pretend they want to help their unwanted relatives, but who really only want them out of the way! I admit that. But I have killed no one!"

"You were in Honolulu at Mr. Soong's house," Chan said. "You and Carleton Sedgwick didn't want me to speak with Angela Farley. You wanted her silenced."

"We were just trying to protect our business here! I went to Hawaii to be sure you didn't know what we were doing, To watch you and to watch Mr. Soong!"

"And what was Carleton Sedgwick doing in Honolulu?" Chan asked quietly.

"He was with me, that's all," Madame Li said.

"Hiding at the Soong mansion? Outside?"

Madame Li stared. "Hiding? No, he wasn't at the house."

"I'm sorry, but he was there," Chan said. "And where is he now?"

"Gone, run away, when he heard you were coming here. He sensed you had found out what we were doing," the woman said. She seemed to think, and her eyes flashed. "Carleton! He did it all, of course! He never trusted Benny not to accidentally reveal our rackets He must have had the heroin sent—"

The lawyer's voice boomed out in the dim temple: *"Liar!"*

They all turned. The tall, elegant lawyer stumbled into the dim temple as if pushed. He had been. Behind him, Lieutenant Forbes walked grimly.

"You were right, Mr. Chan," Forbes said. "We caught him heading south fast in his car. Running like hell."

XVI

CAPTAIN WADE said, "So it was Sedgwick? He killed them all to cover his racket, and the way he was getting his heroin into the country?"

"He was chasing the girl the first night," Forbes stated.

"No!" Carleton Sedgwick cried. "All right, I ran when I heard Charlie Chan was coming down. Why not? I'd called the Farleys, I knew he knew about our racket. But I didn't kill Benny, or Angela, or the Khan! I don't know why they were killed!"

"All were killed," Chan interrupted, "because they had discovered the secret shipment of heroin inside the hidden compartments of the scroll chests. A clever way of shipping drugs; who would investigate elegant boxes containing priceless historical documents sent by a famous amateur scholar and philanthropist to an innocent Temple? Also, if something goes wrong, all eyes would turn to the scrolls as the target of thieves, not to the boxes in which they were carried!"

"Heroin?" Carleton Sedgwick said, startled. "In the boxes?"

"A fact discovered by accident by Benny Chan. Having made that discovery, Benny was confused. Caution told him to say nothing, to pretend he did not know. But loyalty to the Temple and the Khan who helped him made him think he must tell the Khan. The killers saw this, had to stop Benny, so they drowned him!"

"Killers, Charlie?" Captain Wade said. "More than one?"

Chan nodded. "This heroin smuggling is the work of the Yellow Claw Tong. These men wear capes and hats, hide their faces, and looked to Angela Farley like demons! The girl saw them chase Benny Chan that night, grotesque figures in the fog. It is the killers of the Yellow Claw Tong who hung Angela and attacked me in my hotel room. They murdered the Khan when he discovered the secret of the boxes; he, too, doubted Benny Chan died by accident."

C.V. Soong had said nothing for some time, had been listening as if he could not believe what he was hearingo. Now he spoke from the shadows of the flickering blue lights:

"You mean this tong gang used me? Used my

scrolls as a cover to ship heroin?"

"Yes," Chan said. "Someone got the heroin to Honolulu from the Orient, used a secret Chinese chest to ship it to the mainland. The only question now is, who here is working with the Yellow Claw Tong?"

Chan turned to Betty Chan. "Miss Chan, you were born and raised in Chinatown. You married a young man who was a militant Chinese. A young man who vanished. Where is your ex-husband?"

"George?" the girl said, licked at her pretty lips. "Why, I don't know. Mr. Chan. You . . . you don't mean you think that *I* know anything about the Tong?"

"Who would know better than a girl who is Chinese, who works in a bookstore where Chinese culture is paramount?"

"Of course!" C.V. Soong said angrily. "She must be a member of the Tong. Who else would know that Benny was bringing the chests into the country? Benny must have told her about the scrolls, and she saw a way to smuggle the heroin in. Someone had to get it out of the chests unseen, and who better than his sister? Benny would trust her! She probably met him each time, got him off guard, and took out the heroin before it got to the Temple. But the last time he spotted her doing it, so she sent her Tong to kill him!"

Everyone turned to look at the pretty young

girl. She was pale, looking from one to the other. Wade and Forbes moved closer to her.

Chan shook his head slowly, dark eyes hidden. "One strange fact puzzled me all along. It is the key to the mystery. Benny Chan was drowned. The murder was made to look like accident. By a very great stroke of fortune, Benny fell into the ocean without taking the chest and scroll with him! Luckily, he dropped the box on the beach where the police found it, so the scroll was not lost.

"Also, I was attacked in my hotel room, the Khan was murdered, but once again the chest was not taken, and the scroll was safe. Very odd. It would have been a much better accident to Benny if the box were lost in the ocean. When I was attacked and the Khan murdered, it would have seemed again like the motive was the robbery of the scroll, if only the chest or scroll had been taken by the killer.

"This would have been much more confusing and would have given the police no chance to discover the hidden compartment, or the special tracking device used on chest so I could be followed in San Francisco. By leaving the scroll and chest each time, the killers took an unnecessary risk that the truth would be discovered."

No one spoke. They all watched Charlie Chan.

"There is only one answer—the man who planned this whole scheme to deliver heroin is someone to whom the scrolls are of great value. A man who cannot allow the scrolls to be lost, and who cannot allow the scrolls to be hidden! If the scrolls were taken by the killers, even if they were returned to the owner, they could not ever be shown or they would reveal him to be the killer and a smuggler of drugs. No, the only answer to why the chests were left for the police to find is that they would be returned to the rightful owner! No need, then, to hide the scrolls later."

Chan looked at C.V. Soong. "You are the heroin smuggler, the leader of the Yellow Claw Tong! You are the murderer!"

C.V. Soong said, "Don't be ridiculous, Inspector Chan! Is this the way you got your reputation, accusing innocent people? Why would I smuggle heroin? I'm a rich man, much respected."

"Rich men want to remain rich," Chan said dryly. "I think a thorough check in Hawaii will reveal that you have long made money by being a leader of the Tong, the Chinese Mafia. I'm sure we will now find many Tong members who will talk."

"Really, Mr. Chan?" Soong said, and a gun appeared in his hand. "All right, yes, if you check deeply enough you'll find what you say. I had to continue my work, my philanthropy, and I had to have money. I lead the Yellow Claw Tong, but they won't ever tell you that. I tell you now only because it is time for me to go elsewhere anyway. Do not attempt to follow me, you can't stop me."

As they all stood frozen, the old man backed slowly out of the portal of the eerie temple.

"He won't get far," Lieutenant Forbes said. "I've got my men at every gate and roadblocks up everywhere."

Some hours later, Chan and Captain Wade sat in the captain's San Francisco office. Betty Chan had just left, tears in her eyes for her brother, but smiling because she had known he had not died by accident, and she had helped to catch his killer.

Carleton Sedgwick and Madame Li were in cells waiting to be charged for running their illegal racket.

"So your work here is done, Charlie," Captain Wade said. "Will you be staying in San Francisco much longer?"

Chan smiled. "Unfortunately, no. I had hoped to make one or two social calls while I was here, but as an English writer once wrote, 'A policeman's lot is not a happy one'. There is always work to be done."

The captain smiled ruefully, looking at the stack of paperwork on his desk. "Don't I know it," he said.

"Perhaps next time, Mort. Or, if you should ever get to Honolulu—" Chan let it hang

"Thanks Charlie," Captain Wade said. "But I feel bad about your visit being such a bummer. I'd have enjoyed an evening with you—showing you some of the changes in San Francisco since your last trip. I'm afraid this wasn't a very good time for you."

"On the contrary, Mort," Chan responded. "It is enough to stop such parasites as Mr. Soong. It is always a good feeling to know one has put out the spark before the house caught fire."

"Yeah," Wade nodded. "That's one of the benefits of this job."

"The best one," Chan agreed.

Made in the USA
Lexington, KY
10 January 2012